A
SPLENDID
CONSPIRACY

A
SPLENDID
CONSPIRACY

ALBERT COSSERY

Translated from the French by
ALYSON WATERS

A NEW DIRECTIONS BOOK

Originally published by Editions Gallimard / Editions Joelle Losfeld, Paris, France, in 2000, as *Un Complot de Saltimbanques*
Published by arrangement with Editions Galllimard, Editions Joelle Losfeld, Agence Hoffman, Paris, and The Colchie Agency

New Directions gratefully acknowledges the generous support of a Hemingway Grant and a CNL Award:
Cet ouvrage, publié dans le cadre d'un programme d'aide à la publication, bénéficie du soutien du Ministère des Affaires étrangères et du Service Culturel de l'Ambassade de France aux Etats-Unis.
This work, published as part of a program of aid for publication, received support from the French Ministry of Foreign Affairs and the Cultural Services of the French Embassy in the United States.
This work is published with support from the French Ministry of Culture / Centre national du livre.

Translator's Note: Please see page 215.

Manufactured in the United States of America
Published simultaneously in Canada by Penguin Books Canada, Ltd.
New Directions Books are printed on acid-free paper.
First published as a New Directions Paperbook (NDP1176)

Library of Congress Cataloging-in-Publication Data

Cossery, Albert, 1913–2008.
[Complot de saltimbanques. English]
A splendid conspiracy / Albert Cossery ; translated from the French by Alyson Waters.
p. cm. — (New Directions paperbook ; NDP1176)
ISBN 978-0-8112-1779-8 (pbk. : acid-free paper)
I. Waters, Alyson, 1955– II. Title.
PQ2605.O725C613 2010
834'.912—dc22   2009051819

10 9 8 7 6 5 4 3 2 1

New Directions Books are published for James Laughlin
by New Directions Publishing Corporation,
80 Eighth Avenue, New York 10011

A
SPLENDID
CONSPIRACY

: I :

SEATED AT THE CAFÉ TERRACE, Teymour felt as unlucky as a flea on a bald man's head. His entire bearing expressed idleness, morbid emptiness, and a soul-afflicting desolation at this memorable moment when he was rediscovering his home town after six years spent abroad. His surfeit of bad luck conferred a kind of fatal prestige on him, making him resemble a dethroned monarch, victim of collective treason. He had a wild look about him and seemed paralyzed by pain—a suffocating pain that intensified as his gaze attempted, with extreme reluctance, to take in his dull surroundings. It was as if everything he saw had a gift for reinforcing his suffering. From time to time he closed his eyes, and his face assumed an expression of nostalgic ecstasy, as if he were withdrawing into a world of gracious memories to which he was still bound by almost fleshly ties. Rather than bringing him relief, however, these fleeting journeys into the recent past only increased his suffering in contrast to the implacable reality assailing him as soon as he reopened his eyes. He tried to hold back his stinging tears of helplessness and

3

resentment, for, despite his utter despondency, he realized how odd he must look to the few customers scattered about the terrace, all of whom were beginning to observe him with some alarm. He could certainly expect no consolation from these obtuse minds incapable of appreciating the immeasurable torment of his situation. How could he explain to them that the reason for his despair was neither financial ruin nor the loss of a loved one, but simply the sight of his native city and the terrifying prospect of having to stay there until he perished from boredom? A confession of this sort would have no chance of being understood by these boors who obviously thought they were living in an enchanted city. They would never believe there existed other places on earth more delightful than their own town. Teymour envied them their ignorance; they, at least, were not suffering and had neither the desire nor the ability to indulge in comparisons. For him, alas, this was not the case.

He was a young man, some twenty-six years old, dressed with a stylishness that did not bode well in this especially backward provincial town. His clothing was both eccentric and refined; the cut and quality of the fabric signaled an obviously foreign origin. Certain items—his off-white trench coat, for example—could easily have caused him to be mistaken for a tourist were it not for the fact that no tourist had ever strayed into this city since the dawn of its days. In addition to this almost subversive sartorial finery, a great self-assurance was discernible in him, an ease of manner and a distinction that had clearly been acquired across the seas in the company of a privileged race plunged in the pleasures and splendors of great world capitals. To his perceptive compatriots his remarkable air made him as conspicuous as a belly dancer exposing herself on stage. Teymour had not anticipated the perils of such an encounter, and he began to dread the malicious comments that his fabulous attire would surely provoke. Would he be mistaken for one of those new-generation policemen who had descended on the boat that had carried him home as soon as it had touched shore? They, too, wore trench coats—not as well-cut as his, it's true—and that was all it would take to mislead these uncouth provincials. He recalled how the officials had interrogated him in a nasty, suspicious tone of voice, as if he were a notorious assassin and not the son of a notable returning to his country after several years of study abroad. He'd had to pull out his chemical engineering diploma to mollify them and inspire some respect. It was the first time he had made use of it, and he was highly satisfied with the effect it produced on these figures of authority, so full of their own importance. Still, he retained a rather unpleasant memory of the experience, and the thought that he could be mistaken for a member of this sinister crew significantly exacerbated his unhappiness.

Three days had gone by since Teymour's homecoming, but only that morning had he ventured out of his father's house. For three days he had done nothing but bemoan his fate—only the thickness of the walls prevented the sonorous sighs he heaved from seeping outside. At last he arrived at the conclusion that he was acting like a child by trying to delay the inevitable. He had to submit to the awful fate awaiting him, that is, to begin once again to live the life of a mole in his native city—something he could only imagine with terror and trepidation. And so he had embarked on this mournful pilgrimage with the courage of a condemned man heading for the gallows, desperately hoping to find in it some faint glimmer of comfort. Now, however, everything appeared more dismal, more devastating than he could possibly have imagined even in his darkest moments, starting with this café where he had been a regular customer in his youth. At the time, it had been called the "Lighthouse" and in Teymour's memory it had been lavish and extremely chic; he used to strut about it from morning till night in the company of others his age who filled their idle lives by flaunting their brand new erotic knowledge. Where he had once thought he was rubbing shoulders with genuine opulence, he was now alarmed to find a sordid atmosphere. Yet it was still the same café; only the sign was new. It was now called "The Awakening," no doubt because it was located next to a statue that had been erected on the square in a spirit of renewal during his absence. The square itself, he now realized, was nothing but a vast, rectangular wasteland bordered on three sides by tall houses with peeling facades and barred windows suggestive of old abandoned prisons, and on the fourth by the muddy river that ran through the town. Under the gray November sky, the statue—"The Awakening of the Nation"—stood imposingly on its pedestal, addressing its futile call to eternity. It represented a peasant woman in stylized dress, arm extended enthusiastically toward the poor districts across the river as if to denounce the torpor of the residents; in reality, however, she seemed to be lamenting the fact that

6

she had been woken up to see this abomination. Teymour smiled ironically at the presumption of the allegory; not a soul was, or ever would be, awake in this town—which, at its best, was only good for attracting unemployed archeologists. And as he contemplated this incongruous protrusion that had sprung up in the center of the square, he was seized with a new anguish brought on by the frightful surrounding silence. Through some miracle that surely had nothing to do with his having gone suddenly deaf, all the noises of the city, as well as the voices of the customers on the terrace, had lost their previous intensity to become no more than vague murmurs, imperceptible whispers, as if all the sounds he perceived were coming from very far away. The occasional car crossing the square seemed propelled over quilted ground, gears emitting only harmless squeaks as piteous as the distant moans of children. To Teymour, for years accustomed to the fearsome din of huge metropolises, this whisper-filled silence represented the most insidious danger of all; it was proof that this city was going to swallow him up forever, and even his most desperate sighs would remain everywhere unheard. Tears flooded his eyes and he instinctively lowered his head to hide his shame from the other customers. For a moment he remained blind. Then, slowly, as if through a fog, he began to make out the scraggy silhouette of a hen missing half its feathers that had appeared out of nowhere furiously pecking at minuscule grains of dirt embedded in the cracked tiling of the terrace. It was an old, bony hen, survivor of a famine—not the kind served at wedding banquets. Fixed on him, the uneasy gaze of the hen conveyed the hopeless

7

melancholy of a human being. Teymour envisioned himself suddenly transported to another café terrace dotted with pigeons, gazing upon a sunlit triumphal avenue; then, to a square where fountains gushed and white doves flocked; then, to an ocean shore, contemplating a flight of gulls on a luminous summer morning. These images looming out of his glorious past increased the feeling of having fallen low; he groaned beneath the weight of contempt. So, he was now reduced to the level of that scrawny hen! He chased it away with a clumsy kick; it cackled spitefully and fluttered off, leaving one of its feathers on the tiles.

Teymour was the only son of one of the city's most notable families; his father, a landowner, was quite well-to-do and had always lived off private means, never suspecting that anyone in his family could possibly work. This intelligent outlook owed nothing to some great knowledge of philosophy; old Teymour had almost no education whatsoever. It was but instinct that had guided him in this judicious choice. He loved life, and above all he loved his family too much to see them work. Nevertheless, somewhat belatedly—perhaps his daily reading of the paper had made him concerned about the transformations taking place in the world—the ludicrous idea had come into his head of seeing his son get a degree; and—the height of ambition!—a degree in chemical engineering, merely because of some stock he owned in the sugar refinery that was the city's sole industry. This request, so late in coming, would probably have been rejected by the party in question had Teymour not seen in his father's vanity a means of spending a few years abroad where, he knew from reliable sources, fascinating pleasures and lasciviousness reigned supreme. Like all young men trapped in their provinces, he had dreamed of leading a dissolute life. The opportunity had at last been given to him to verify the enchanting rumors about the abundance of vice in certain Western capitals. He had not been disappointed.

From the very outset of his stay abroad, he had to admit that he never could have imagined such magnificent debauchery. Amazed by the variety of sensual pleasures, the multitude of temptations, he devoted himself furiously to them all, continually putting off his tiresome studies. Even had he wanted to, he couldn't have found enough spare time for any serious activity. Little by little he managed to persuade himself that it would be a waste of his time and his youth to study all those absurd subjects destined to turn him into a functionary. Consequently, he had not enrolled in any university, had not bought a single chemistry book; instead he had purchased a stylish and costly wardrobe that was indispensable to his taste for show. During endless nights he had made love to sublime women and experienced emotions and adventures of all kinds. A few months of this glorious existence had sufficed to make him forget he was there to earn a degree, except on those rare occasions when he received a letter from his father worrying about the state and progress of his learning. This call to order mortified Teymour for a few hours; then he got caught up once again in the pulse of his new life and thought no more about it.

As the years went by and old Teymour did not see his son return, he began to be troubled by the snail's pace of these interminable studies; he did not understand how it could take so much time and money to get a degree, even one in chemical engineering. Knowing nothing of studies of this kind, he imagined all sorts of things, and did not dare seek advice from others for fear of provoking their animosity. But a day came when his patience ran out, and then the letters he sent his son became more and more severe, ordering him to return home without delay or his funds would be cut off. Old Teymour was loath to resort to this kind of blackmail, but he was forced into it by the pressing need to put an end to this interminable situation. He had bragged so much to everyone about his son's scholarly success that, as the years dragged on and this son did not reappear, people began to wonder if he had died. Though they remained within the bounds of common courtesy, they demonstrated by meaningful nods that they were not fooled. The dignified old man no longer knew how to respond when asked, with an irony not devoid of pity, for news of his illustrious offspring. Furthermore, he had already schemed to obtain a position at the sugar refinery for the young engineer, and the perpetual absence of the prospective job candidate would in the end turn into a scandal. This last and most important reason had led him to the only reprisal available to him to speed the return of this neglectful son, whom he now regretted having consigned to self-destruction in dubious lands so ravaged by debauchery.

Crushed by this paternal ultimatum, Teymour found himself obliged to pack his bags and say farewell to the pleasant life that had been shaped around his ambitions.

But it wasn't so simple. Before heading home, he had to obtain a diploma from somewhere; he couldn't possibly stand before his father empty-handed. Having known for some time that he could acquire one for a fee, he set about searching for this cursed piece of paper and, after many discreet efforts, he bought one, in due form—as lovely as a real one—for an exorbitant sum that immediately reduced him to the level of a pauper. He had to travel back third class on a boat belonging to a second-rate company that treated its passengers like convicts, if not galley-slaves. During this difficult passage, he'd had plenty of time to prepare himself for the slow and barbaric death awaiting him in his home town. The boat, practically adrift, seemed never to find a port of any kind. Every now and again Teymour would take the diploma out of his suitcase and examine it attentively, trying to detect an error, a defect, or an oversight that would have made it unusable. But each time the diploma passed his inspection with flying colors; it seemed even too perfect for what he planned to do with it. He would then let out a sigh of relief and place it back in his suitcase. This, at least, was something solid, the only concrete thing to come out of these six years of so-called studies that no one would have the impertinence to contest. Rather than alarming him, his total ignorance of the rudiments of chemistry seemed, on the contrary, an advantage, for it meant he had no chance of giving himself away by spouting nonsense. He was determined to behave modestly and not boast about his knowledge. Not even the engineering job at the sugar refinery—about which his dotard of a father had told him with such delight in his last letter as an incitement to come home—could, he felt, expose him: his cynical, sardonic nature had always prevented him from believing that jobs existed that demanded real competence. According to Teymour, no one was competent. Any imbecile could easily display a genuine diploma; that wasn't the main thing. The main thing was to act like someone who *knows* but who is loath to divulge his knowledge, at least in front of subordinates. As for his future colleagues, he was sure they knew no more than he did; he, however, had a definite advantage over them—his imagination. These comforting thoughts kept him company for the duration of his journey.

Old Teymour was so moved on seeing his son who had become an engineer—or so he believed—that he practically stammered with affection; he could hardly wait to finish his outpourings before asking Teymour to show him the diploma he had traveled so far to obtain. The old man was eager to see it with his own eyes. Teymour complied and tendered the thin, rolled-up parchment to his father with the hint of respect owed to a dignitary to whom one is offering a priceless gift. The old man accepted it with equal respect, unrolling it very carefully, then putting on his glasses to decipher this treasure brought from afar as testimony to his son's learning. He spent a long time poring over it, his face slowly taking on an expression of infinite dismay; he seemed to find it ridiculous that a piece of paper that was not even gilded could have demanded so much effort and, above all, such considerable expense. Apparently, he was disappointed by the format of the diploma, as if he had been expecting a document of this sort to be at least a meter long, with words of praise for *him* printed on it. Old Teymour believed, and rightly so, that he had had something to do with the acquisition of this diploma, and now he felt he had been deliberately left out of the whole thing. He was humiliated by this piece of paper with its elaborate and illegible signatures and its typographical austerity. He pulled at it from both ends, trying in vain to stretch it; the diploma resisted, remaining immutable. Faced with the inertia of this precious material, old Teymour was forced to give up, fearing that a tear would only increase its frailty. He let out a sigh of disbelief and looked at his son with commiseration.

"It isn't very big," he said. "I hope you haven't forgotten everything you've learned. This piece of paper cost me a fortune."

Teymour remained silent; he almost pitied his father. But a mad hope led him to say:

"Father, if you'd like, I can get a bigger one, but I'll need to go back there for a few more years."

"Oh, no, this one will do!" cried old Teymour. "After all, it seems suitable enough for our city. But I don't like how pale you look. You must have worked very hard all those years. Rest up, and in a few days you can go to the factory. They're waiting. I've arranged everything. They're all curious to see you on the job."

And now, revisiting this scene in his mind, Teymour had the sense that it belonged to some absurd dream. He tried to convince himself that he was sleeping, and that a day would come when he would awake, freed from this oppressive nightmare. He closed his eyes for a long time to create the illusion necessary for the miracle to occur. When he opened them again, an astonishing sight appeared before him. For a few moments he remained dumbfounded, trying to make out the strange, brightly colored group that stood out from the surrounding gray and that, coming from the far end of the square, advanced in slow motion toward the café. Pulled by a bony horse, an old carriage seemed on the verge of collapse beneath the weight of several females in ceremonial dress who filled it to the brim. It was moving forward with difficulty—either it was going for a very slow drive or the cabby did not dare whip his horse for fear of killing it. It took forever for the conveyance to arrive in front of the café terrace, where Teymour could study at close range the girls in their sequined dresses with plunging necklines, lolling about, laughing and gesturing in the grip of the hysteria of masquerade. It was hard to tell how many there were—they were stuck to one other, making up a mountain of flesh and fabric with flashes of sequin and cheap jewelry. From this pile of festive creatures emerged a motionless and terrifying face—a hybrid monster, neither man nor woman, covered entirely in white powder as if to erase any and all human expression beneath a plaster mask. Its blazing black eyes were unfathomable and empty, like the eyes of the dead made up for eternity. It remained stiff and haughty, indifferent to the deluge of feigned rejoicing that was making the carriage tremble. Teymour was momentarily captivated by this face of an opulent ogress taking her lively victims to her den; then he turned his gaze away and brought it to rest on a girl—the youngest and most beautiful in the group—

14

who, on the seat near the cabby, was wearing a dress of almost transparent pink tulle. She had got hold of the whip and was brandishing it above her head while emitting the cries of a female in heat being serviced by a giant. The queen of this magnificent mob, she seemed as amazing and outrageous as a vision glimpsed in an erotic dream.

The carriage went by, grazing the edges of the terrace; it drove around the entire square and, after a time, came back to the café. The whole thing resembled a circus parade. The girls' gaudy dresses shone with the thousand flames of their sequins, coating the dismal landscape of the square with a brilliant, fluid stain as illusory as a mirage. Teymour noticed that the customers around him had stood up, the better to savor the glorious spectacle of bared flesh crammed into the carriage, these girls who were rewarding the men's vanity by calling to them and ogling them with fiery eyes. Other customers came out of the dining hall and remained on the threshold, struck dumb with admiration and lust. Teymour heard exclamations and husky sighs of an animal sensuality, mixed with obscene jeers. The object of this passionate display was the girl beside the cabby; she was now standing up and performing a kind of belly dance that was having the most potent effect on the virility of those men who, a moment before, had seemed dazed by a millennial drowsiness. Suddenly they began to applaud and cheer the young dancer. As if in response to their frenzied cries, she accentuated the swaying of her hips, lifted her dress, thrust forward her juvenile tummy in a shameless, lascivious gesture, then stuck out her tongue several times as if to defy love. An enormous, liberating wave of sound swept over the terrace. "Now that's what I call Awakening the Nation!" thought Teymour as the carriage pulled away and disappeared around the corner of the square. Giddy, forgetting his own misery, he retained from the extraordinary spectacle only the pale face of the madame, sitting like an implacable monster in the midst of her menagerie. Against his will he shivered, as if recalling some evil beast.

The waiter was standing near him, livid, still under the shock of his contact with this lust-on-wheels. Teymour couldn't help asking:

"What on earth was that?"

"Where have you been, Excellency! Haven't you heard about Wataniya's brothel? It's the poshest in the city."

"Sorry. I've been out of the country for quite some time."

"Ah, I see," said the waiter, looking at Teymour attentively. "Well, nowadays it's the custom. Every time Wataniya attracts a new recruit, she hires a carriage and parades the new girl through the city with the old ones. That way, potential customers can size up the merchandise—it's called advertising."

He expressed himself fervently; his jaded gaze reflected a kind of sordid and resigned eroticism.

"What progress!" said Teymour. "In my day, nothing like that existed. Thanks for the information."

"At your service, Excellency! Believe me, you won't be bored here. Did you see that little whore, the one exhibiting herself beside the cabby? She's the new girl—not even fifteen. To look at her, you'd think she was the daughter of a government minister."

The waiter glanced one last time at the spot where the carriage had disappeared, and his sly face became sullen and sad, as if he were wistful about all those fleshly lures that had escaped his concupiscence. Then, with a strident voice calling him from the dining room, he left Teymour to fret over the comments he had made about the girl. Why would the young whore be a minister's daughter? It was a while before he recalled that the expression was a common one, used to enhance the value of people or things by comparing them to a high-ranking personage. The fact that he had forgotten this mortified him, and he realized just how impervious to this city and the colorful language of its inhabitants he had become. His mortification increased all the more at the idea that the brothel run by that frightening creature Wataniya would be his sole distraction from now on. Admittedly during his long stay abroad he had, on occasion, visited all kinds of brothels, but it was out of sheer intellectual curiosity rather than from necessity; whereas here it would no doubt be one of the rare pleasures—perhaps the only one—within his grasp, the sole possibility of joy to which he could aspire. Suddenly he felt so sorry for himself that he decided to go back to the house.

This fainthearted resolution did not last long, however; before shutting himself up at home, he had to find Medhat, a childhood friend about whom he had not ceased thinking all these years. In fact, Teymour's only reason for going out that morning had been to see Medhat, even though he kept postponing the moment when he would find himself face to face with his old friend; his behavior was due both to the anxiety this reunion was causing him and to a feeling of guilt. During the early period following his departure, he had written Medhat a few tedious letters about his health and his deep contentment; then he had stopped writing—not deliberately, but almost unwittingly, so caught up had he become in the constant exaltation and euphoria of discovering a new world. But Teymour's superb detachment—which had stemmed from an unconscious desire to destroy all concrete ties to the past—had never implied a fading of his affection for this far-away friend. Each episode in his adventurous life, each pleasure experienced through a chance encounter, each minute of some unusual and wonderful situation, had only had meaning because Teymour could already picture himself recounting it to Medhat. It was the complicity he conferred on his friend who had stayed behind that had given weight to his most insignificant adventures, and shaded them with tender melancholy. But now that he was at long last in a position to relate every detail of the passionate life he had led over there, he wondered if Medhat were capable of imagining, or even of understanding through mere reason, such breathtaking things. Would Medhat even believe him? Could he possibly conceive of the blissful wonders that had been offered to Teymour? Just as daylight cannot be explained to a blind man, wouldn't his words come up against a void of incredulity? He realized that no power of language would be able to describe, even approximately, the Edenic existence that a paternal decree had brutally brought to an end. But if Medhat couldn't understand him, who, then, would listen to him in this city? Like the bearer of some implausible piece of news who has little chance of being believed, Teymour feared he would be taken for a braggart. The nature of his knowledge was so enormous, so unheard-of in these regions, that he thought it would be better to keep silent if he didn't want to spark a riot. He was like a man several centuries ahead of his compatriots, obliged to keep to himself his knowledge of an invention of immeasurable importance.

And so it was with some trepidation that Teymour prepared himself for this meeting with his old friend. In what state of moral decrepitude would he find Medhat? He knew vaguely the Medhat was working for the local newspaper, that he had married, and that he had even had a child. Teymour found this information, obtained from domestic sources, surprising and thought it indicated a regrettable decline of Medhat's intellectual faculties, to say the least. Had Medhat perhaps become a civil servant, a petty bourgeois bogged down in a provincial routine, a gloomy soul doomed to insignificance? This possibility was not to be excluded, for who could resist this city's annihilating atmosphere? Yet Teymour had difficulty reconciling the image of Medhat, married and head of household, with the young man with a splendid sense of humor he had known, whose only goal had been to hunt down ephemeral, undiscovered pleasures in this stinking necropolis. Medhat had been the only one among the friends of Teymour's youth with whom he had been able to form a bond of unfailing complicity based on an acknowledgment of their shared taste for a pointless and joyful life. He still remembered their mad thirst for thrills, their mania for inventing, despite the aridity of a hostile territory, all kinds of elaborate projects for the sole purpose of having a good time. It had been really such a pitiful era, and yet grandiose, too, because managing to have a good time was for them a real feat. Teymour hoped that Medhat had, after all these years, been able to keep intact his mischievous spirit and his devilish ability to discern a delicious detail even in a cartload of trash. In fact, this rash hope had never left Teymour; Medhat was absolutely vital for surviving the misfortune striking him. Yet his desire to believe in the unchanging character of his old friend was on occasion tinged with mortal fear. At those moments, it seemed to Teymour that he had arrived too late and that Medhat's mind had already been infected by the revolting mold eating away at the city.

The sound of a voice coming from the next table made him start; he turned his head slightly to see a customer who looked like a well-to-do peasant speaking with gentle authority to the waiter. He was a middle-aged man, still very dashing, enveloped in a loose-fitting black wool caftan lavishly embroidered with gold thread at the collar and sleeves, and wearing a spotless white turban; his enormous mustache with its turned-up tips, dyed an ochre color, seemed false, as if he were trying to conceal his identity. It was too heavy for his face, and this absurd adornment reminded Teymour of a surrealist painting. In order to pay for his drink, the man had opened and placed before him a fat goat-skin wallet bloated with bank notes, and he ostentatiously let it remain on the table as witness to his total solvency. The waiter responded with touching obsequiousness and bowed to him as if he were a great feudal lord visiting the dregs of his kingdom. Despite the convoluted structure of their conversation, Teymour grasped that the man was looking for amusement. He was utterly astonished.

When the waiter left, the man put his swollen wallet back in the pocket of his caftan, then turned to Teymour and said, with the courtesy of a noble traveler asking for information from a high-ranking native:

"Do you live here? My god!"

"Yes," sighed Teymour.

"You are so lucky!" said the man, for whom Teymour's sigh seemed filled with contentment. "Allow me to envy you. I live in the country; I only come here on business from time to time. What a beautiful city!"

Teymour did not answer; holding a discussion about the beauty of the city with this poor ignoramus was, given the circumstances, equivalent to suicide. He simply nodded his head with a pained, tragic air, as if this mute agreement had been dragged out of him by a torturer.

"Today is my lucky day," said the man as he got up. "I intend to take advantage of the pleasures of the city before going back to the country. Peace be with you!"

He walked away with the determined steps of someone about to paint the town red, and with a confidence that nothing, not even a desert, could demoralize.

Teymour was making every effort to pierce the mystery of this robust optimism when, once again, he was drawn from his thoughts by a charming and unexpected sight. This time it was not a carriage transporting delirious females, but a simple bicycle ridden by a fourteen-year-old girl who burst into the square at top speed. Decked out like a *saltimbanque*, the girl was wearing a flesh-colored maillot that hugged her body and was cinched at the waist with a belt of red fabric; a short tunic of dark-red velvet decorated with sequins clung to her youthful bust, allowing the tiny mounds of her breasts to be glimpsed beneath the maillot. Her makeup was but two pink spots on her cheeks and turquoise eye shadow, giving her impassive face the appearance of a mechanical doll. The young street entertainer pedaled effortlessly, relaxed and graceful, swaying every which way, letting go of the handlebars occasionally and crossing her arms, maintaining control of her machine with small motions of her legs. When she was a few meters from the café, she slowed down and began to make circles and figure eights, maneuvering inside a smaller and smaller area until at last she came to a halt, locking her wheels, in a wobbly equilibrium. Then, suddenly, she took off again, carefree. When she passed in front of Teymour, she smiled and made a sign of welcome, as if she had just recognized in him a dear friend for whom she had been waiting a very long time. Teymour, surprised and delighted, returned her greeting, but the young saltimbanque had already soared away on her bicycle. He searched with his eyes in every nook and cranny of the square, hoping to see her loom unexpectedly back into view; he clung to this fleeting apparition like a castaway to the smallest bit of flotsam. In the girl's warm smile he had made out a hidden, tender, familial complicity. Whatever happened from then on, he knew that some tiny shard of joy lay concealed for him in the dark recesses of this city. He got up and left the café, haunted by this magical memory as if by some vague promise of happiness. As he approached the statue, he had the curiosity to study the stylized peasant woman standing on her pedestal. Examined at close range, she brought to mind a beseeching creature whose raised arm seemed to accuse invisible executioners. Teymour admired the skill of the sculptor who had managed to incorporate obvious and terrible oppression in the stone's curves. For anyone at all sensitive to irony, the artist had left behind an ingenious message. Teymour's heart overflowed with gratitude for this anonymous humorist who must have had some good laughs, making this piece that the government had commissioned.

Teymour started over the metal bridge across the river; after a few steps, he stopped to breathe in the damp, cool air filled with the scent of the sea. Overloaded feluccas with white triangle sails were moving slowly over the muddy water, rekindling in him the rapture of departures. On the bank he had just left, massively ugly detached homes flaunted their pathetic luxury in front of the opposite bank where, beyond the shoreline flecked with palm trees, stretched the poorer district with its tumbledown hovels, its shacks, and its filthy alleyways. It was in this wretched part of the city that Medhat, in the spirit of revolt against the bleak conformism of the wealthier neighborhoods, had set up house shortly before Teymour had left the country. Teymour hastened across the bridge, spurred by the belief that in this poorer quarter some traces of boisterous life perhaps might remain; he hadn't forgotten that the masses are always more amusing than their masters. Unfortunately, his hopes were misplaced; there was no liveliness of any kind in this tangle of rickety houses and deserted alleys. The silence was even more impressive here: it was the ritual silence of poverty, in which the slightest sound took on a tragic resonance. The few open shops were plunged in darkness and it was impossible to guess what they were selling since there was no visible sign of merchandise. A solitary, mangy nanny goat followed Teymour with the persistence of a prostitute, coming to rub lasciviously against his leg, as if she were accustomed to fornicating with men. It was in the company of this charming young lady that Teymour headed toward his old friend's home, being careful not to lose his way.

: II :

STRETCHED OUT FULLY CLOTHED on his bed, Medhat was smiling mischievously as he thought of his friend Teymour and how he was about to welcome him into his home. He was far from giving in to the excitement that this reunion ordinarily would have aroused in him. For three days he had been expecting Teymour to appear from one moment to the next and recite his tales of woe. He knew him well enough to be certain that, at this very moment, Teymour was turning his misery over in his mind, believing himself exiled to his own town. And so, Medhat had promised himself not to allude to those six years his friend had spent out of the country and to behave as if this long stretch of time had never existed. He had absolutely no desire to hear the whining of a man stupid enough to fall under the picturesque spell of distant lands. The picturesque bored Medhat. He had an inherent scorn for that mass of fidgety, travel-crazed humanity always running after happiness but in reality only managing to run in circles, incapable of catching anything but a virus. This scorn stemmed from deep instinct rather than from any kind of criticism of society; it had been years since Medhat had any interest in reforming his fellow man. He had better things to do. The battle he was waging was a personal one, renewed on a daily basis, its sole purpose to turn to his advantage a small scrap of the joy that, often unpredictable and difficult to recognize, had been lost among men. With this simple and fundamentally realistic moral code, he managed to be perfectly happy anywhere and everywhere; for Medhat, no place had more of a claim to happiness than any other. And his friend Teymour was not about to prove the contrary by recounting his adventures abroad. Every country has its share of imbeciles, bastards, and whores. You had to be a fool to believe that bigger and better things were happening elsewhere. The only thing that changed was the language spoken; everywhere the same imbeciles, the same bastards, and the same whores could be found expressing the same things in different languages: the novelty consisted of nothing more. Medhat refused to forgive the absurdity and madness of people who learned all kinds of foreign tongues simply to grasp the meaning of the same idiotic remarks they could hear at home for free. He, for one, had never been tempted to trot the globe looking for experiences that were supposed to be transcendent because they took place in distant hemispheres. What was the purpose of changing continents, longing for other surroundings, if you were not even capable of seeing what was around you? Medhat had no reason to criticize the town where he'd spent his whole life. Beneath its deceptive and admittedly depressing appearance were concealed great gifts of madness and murderous rage capable of competing with any world capital. To be convinced of this fact one needed only not to be blind.

His gaze rested mechanically on the child playing on the bedroom floor with an empty cookie box, and he smiled as he imagined Teymour's coming upon this domestic scene. In truth the child was not his; he had married the mother when she was already pregnant—an eccentric decision on his part. Two years earlier, an elderly worker from the sugar refinery—a good man whom Medhat knew and who lived in his neighborhood—had come to him and confided that one of his daughters, barely nubile, had been impregnated by a municipal street sweeper who had since absconded without a trace. To avoid dishonor the old man could think of nothing but to kill his daughter. He was a peaceful and good-natured fellow, however, not at all a brute, and his role as avenger was repellent to him. Believing Medhat to be the only educated person in the neighborhood, he had wanted to consult him about this sad business. Medhat was pained by the old man's distress and, sensing the perilous nature of this discussion, tried persistently to change the man's mind about such a macabre undertaking. The old fellow was deaf to the young man's advice and did nothing but shake his head and repeat again and again that something must be done quickly because scandal was knocking at his door. The situation was all the more pitiful in that the poor wretch did not even own a knife with which to carry out his plan. He was still waiting, crouching on the ground, staring at Medhat with eyes red from trachoma as if at an oracle. Suddenly a crazy idea came to Medhat, a dangerously optimistic idea but one that seemed to him to be the sole solution acceptable to this dishonored father. He would marry the girl, arrange a wedding feast, and invite all his friends and acquaintances. He would have a wonderful evening to look forward to and, even better, an unhoped-for opportunity to escape his routine: a wedding—his own—now, there was something completely unpredictable in the realm of delights! The old man thought he was joking when Medhat offered to become his son-in-law, but after endless discussion, he left holding his head high, convinced that his entire family had just miraculously climbed the social ladder.

The wedding took place a week later, in the best popular tradition, with a bridal procession, musicians, and a banquet that lasted until dawn. Medhat had never intended to exercise his conjugal rights; he was only thinking of saving an old man from dishonor and, at the same time, planning the wedding to amuse himself. His apartment had two rooms so he had let the girl have one while she awaited the birth of her child; afterward, he intended to repudiate her with dignity. But circumstances caused him to act otherwise. In the first place, the girl was rather attractive and she showed her gratitude with boundless adoration and obedience. She was still a little girl who would stare wide-eyed at the luxury of her new home because, compared to her parents' sordid shack, the splendor of her husband's lodgings dazzled her. Medhat had felt too ill-at-ease to explain that he had married her just for the heck of it. During the months of her pregnancy, he grew so accustomed to her presence that he no longer wanted to send her away, and when she gave birth, he kept both her and the child. Now she had grown up and was practically a woman; she had even proved to be a very good housewife. Medhat did not regret the wild idea he had had one day merely to satisfy his love of parties; he was even tempted to sing his own praises. As it turned out, his marriage delighted him; he spent many agreeable hours playing with both mother and child.

The child threw down the empty cookie box and began to moan softly, waving his hands in Medhat's direction as if to remind him of his paternal responsibilities. But Medhat, who was still preoccupied with the unexpected return of his friend Teymour, appeared to take no notice. The fact that Teymour had stayed away for six years, parading around foreign capitals, seemed as unexceptional to Medhat as if he had been living all that time in a neighboring village. He couldn't imagine showing the slightest consideration to someone because of a mere question of distance; this would have been like rewarding ignorance. From the very outset Medhat had been stunned by Teymour's departure; he saw the move as a childish, almost infantile, defect. What was it Teymour had hoped to find by going away? His leaving was not only a betrayal of Medhat, it was also the negation of their shared idea of pleasure, which consisted of enjoying life in all its most basic and ludicrous manifestations. And where on earth were such ingredients more numerous and more obvious than in this very city where at every step the bizarre and the humdrum seemed spontaneously to cross paths? Such a coalition of fundamental absurdities and vain idiocies was not to be found elsewhere. At times Medhat wondered if these enigmatic human beings, these creatures with their unsuspected ways of thinking who moved around him, were part of a living reality or an imagined one—so easily did their actions attain a kind of outrageous lunacy. He had always had the foresight to be at the center of a mysterious and unfathomable universe, more captivating than any other. Having no ambitions of the material sort, thumbing his nose at money and honors, he had found a way to lead a life that cost him little but was rich in leisure, allowing him to increase his already profound knowledge of his city. His contributions to the local newspaper were reduced to one or two articles a month on the destitution of the sugar refinery workers, written in a satiric, provocative tone for which he had acquired a reputation as a subversive. He was not unaware that he was being monitored by the chief of police, who took him for a fearsome conspirator. He reveled in the ineffable absurdity of the authorities' distrust, for if Medhat did any conspiring whatsoever, it was not with a political aim, but rather always in the hope of creating an amusement of some sort. At the very moment the chief of police was suspecting him of concocting the most horrid plots against the government, Medhat was using every marvel of ingenuity and patience with the aim of debauching a girl whose parents kept her on a very short leash. He could often be found whispering in his friends' ears, running around the city with a dubious purpose and a secretive air, or stopping for hours beneath a *porte-cochère* staring at a window in a house across the way. His every move was noted in high places as if its aim were to bring down the regime. Medhat had been fueling this misunderstanding for years, and he got extraordinary satisfaction from it, the likes of which Teymour could never have known abroad. But no doubt that fool was now impervious to the humor of such a situation and was luxuriating in an exorbitant melancholy that could interfere with their future relations. For this reason, Medhat was determined to take away Teymour's martyr's crown by refusing to listen to his grievances. He was yanked from his daydreams when Nuri entered the bedroom.

"Lunch is ready," she said.

Nuri seemed hardly to have outgrown childhood. Dressed becomingly in a cotton shift with a pattern of bright yellow flowers, her hair concealed beneath a black net kerchief, she was wearing with remarkable dignity an array of fake gold and colored-glass jewelry which gave her the appearance of a young sultana who had magically materialized inside a poor man's home to bring it affluence and prosperity. All these trinkets were scarcely worth a few piasters and were gifts from Medhat, who loved to see her thus adorned with mock riches. She remained motionless, in an attitude of total submission, with her eyes lowered as if gratitude forbade her from looking her husband in the face. This behavior annoyed Medhat who had not yet managed to free her from the sense of her sin and her feeling of indebtedness to him. No matter how often he repeated that she owed him nothing, that he had married her because he was madly in love with her, she remained obstinate in her noxious gratitude. Medhat jumped to the foot of the bed, took the child in his arms and lifted him in the air several times. The child stopped moaning and smiled contentedly.

"I'm going to make him into a monkey trainer," he said to the young woman. "What do you think of that?"

"Whatever you like," answered Nuri. "You are the master."

Medhat placed the child on the floor; then, as if he had just realized he was late for an important rendezvous, he raced toward the door.

"I've got to go," he cried to the young woman. "Don't wait lunch for me."

He was practically running as he left the house. He had lost all this time waiting for Teymour, and now because of that renegade he would probably be too late for his meeting. He was hurrying, full of rancor against his childhood friend, when he saw him zigzagging along the alleyway, looking dazed, as if trying to find his way through a maze. The sight made Medhat's heart skip a beat and for a second he stopped, wonderfully dumbfounded. All his love for Teymour came bursting forth at once. Teymour had not yet recognized him; he was coming toward Medhat, groping about like a blind man. Medhat took a deep breath and feigned total nonchalance. He went up to Teymour as if he had seen him the previous day, and, taking his arm and pulling him along, said:

"Ah, here you are at last! We will just make it!"

This cavalier greeting flabbergasted Teymour. He let himself be carried along by Medhat, appalled by his monstrous indifference. Medhat had not seen him in six years, and yet he was greeting him as if he had never left the country, not asking about his health, not even seeming surprised to see him again. Such behavior was insulting at the very least, but Teymour felt no anger whatsoever, so outrageous did this conduct seem.

"Where are you dragging me?"

"You'll see," answered Medhat. "We have to hurry. We'll be late."

Medhat had a mischievous smile and the feverishness of someone about to miss an extraordinary event. He wasn't looking at Teymour. He was pulling him by the arm while guiding him across potholes and puddles. Teymour was too stunned to react to this pressure, this haste toward an unknown goal. He followed Medhat without the slightest resistance, his spirit obeying a kind of imperious fatalism. Medhat's strange behavior made Teymour suspicious but, at the same time, it was somehow reassuring. Medhat had not changed in the least. He had always had a penchant for mystery and conspiracy—but still, what was keeping him from showing a minimum of civility toward a friend whom he was seeing again after such a long absence? This was the only thing that remained incomprehensible to Teymour, and he was angry at Medhat for having transformed a happy reunion into this ridiculous race through horrid back streets full of refuse and waste of all sorts.

The lecherous nanny goat was standing guard at the corner of an alley; she cast a languorous glance at Teymour, started to come toward him, then stopped, hesitant.

Without turning to his companion, Medhat asked:

33

"Have you met that goat?"

"I haven't had the pleasure, but she followed me for a while on her own initiative. I had a hard time chasing her away."

"Congratulations."

"For what?"

"She's our neighborhood whore. And you've already won her heart. She must have been very impressed by your lovely attire. Careful she doesn't graze on your raincoat. She adores imported fabric."

This first allusion to his stay abroad devastated Teymour; besides the facile irony, he perceived in it a note of contemptuous antagonism. Medhat seemed extremely amused by his helplessness and distress. He was pulling him along faster and faster as if they were threatened by some danger. The nanny goat dawdled at a distance.

They crossed the bridge at top speed and once again Teymour saw the square with its horrid houses and the peasant woman standing on her pedestal, arm stretched their way as if exposing them to public condemnation. Nothing had budged. Yet Teymour was no longer gripped by the anguish he had felt in the early morning when he had sat alone at the café terrace; it was as if Medhat's presence had brought a tiny hint of optimism to his vision, a glimmer of faint joy. The square had lost its frightening appearance; in his eyes it had become simply mediocre, just like when he was young and he and Medhat had wandered through the city streets driven by their appetite for bawdy adventures without any concern for the setting of their exploits. It seemed to Teymour that he could breathe more easily, and that the immense weight bearing down on his chest had lifted for good, leaving behind a kind of touching curiosity about this city slumbering beneath its ugliness. And, oddly, he suddenly had a premonition of everything that was hidden beneath these despicable surfaces; for the first time he looked around him at the square, the houses, and the ridiculous statue with the delighted fascination of a man contemplating treasures once lost, now found again.

This abrupt change in his state of mind gave him the courage to stop and pull his arm from Medhat's grip. Medhat turned and stared at him in amazement.

"What's the matter? Come on, let's go. We're very late."

"Late for what?"

"You'll see. I don't have time to explain. It's a very important matter."

"Can you at least tell me where we're going?"

"To The Awakening. That's all. What did you think?"

Teymour nodded and, resigned, followed Medhat to the café terrace. Almost all the tables were now occupied by lively customers in the middle of pointless, never-ending discussions, their laughter and colorful profanities audible all around. Teymour was very surprised by this; then he recalled that it was after noon and as a result the city's residents could, without demeaning themselves, respond to the statue's call. So, there *was* an hour of the day when the nation awoke. Teymour took comfort in this thought, and with the pitiful smile of someone recovering from a coma, but not yet fully conscious, on seeing his loved ones for the first time, he turned confidently toward his companion.

Once he had carefully inspected the terrace, Medhat exclaimed with a hint of scorn:

"The wretch! He's not here yet! Come on, let's sit down."

They sat at an empty table at the terrace edge and ordered coffee without sugar as if they were at a wake. Medhat remained silent, but he was visibly irritated and continually shot furious glances toward a corner of the square where the mysterious character for whom he was waiting was no doubt expected to appear. He seemed to be paying no attention whatsoever to Teymour who, although burning to ask questions, refrained from doing so, knowing it was futile to try such a tactic with his friend. He had to bide his time and allow Medhat to reveal his secret when he tired of playing the conspirator. With the detachment of a disillusioned reveler (a most striking attitude, which he had perfected abroad), Teymour too began to watch that corner of the square. The importance Medhat attached to his meeting seemed huge, given the way he had raced here and his disappointment on not seeing the person he was looking for. What kind of man was he waiting for then, and for what reasons? Without knowing why, Teymour began to grow anxious about the unknown person's tardiness.

What if this meeting were a prelude to a real conspiracy? There was nothing implausible about this rather absurd hypothesis. Teymour had learned from his father about the rumors surrounding Medhat because of his contacts with the sugar refinery workers. People claimed that it was at Medhat's secret directives that the majority of the strikes were being fomented. Marrying the daughter of a worker had given these rumors serious foundation; it was intimated that there were political motives behind Medhat's having married beneath his station. All this small-town gossip seemed terribly overblown to Teymour. He thought he knew Medhat well enough to ignore all this nonsense. But what was happening at the moment confused and distressed him. Could it be that Medhat, by sheer chance, had discovered a new form of amusement in eminently dangerous intrigues? It wasn't impossible. Once he started down the path of some entertaining adventure, Medhat could not be stopped, even if that path led to troubles of the worst kind. The problem, however, was that Teymour did not envision himself having returned to his home town to stir up strikes. He hadn't foreseen the possibility of such a calamity.

These thoughts led him to observe his friend's behavior with suspicion. Medhat still seemed in the grip of some inner agitation, but the nature of his feverishness had changed; now it was like the impatience of a lover worried about his mistress's delay. With furtive gestures he smoothed his eyebrows, straightened his tie, ran his hands through his hair like a common womanizer getting ready to pounce on his prey. Once he'd finished this perfunctory primping, he sat bolt upright in his chair and struck a flattering pose, legs crossed, head thrown back, a vague, love-struck look in his eyes. While Teymour was wondering about the meaning of this little game, he saw a group of young schoolgirls file in front of the terrace, one uglier than the next, decked out in yellow canvas smocks with their schoolbags slung across their shoulders like beggars' pouches. They made up a pathetic cross-section of the female race, and Teymour wondered in horror if it were to dazzle these ugly young girls that Medhat had pulled out his full bag of seducer's tricks. He was in the process of being highly offended by this patent lack of taste when suddenly Medhat seemed ready to leap from his chair; he gripped Teymour's arm and whispered in an overexcited voice:

"Look! Here they come!"

"They" were two splendid fifteen- or sixteen-year-old girls, braids rolled on top of their heads like tiaras, their dignified style and bearing in sharp contrast to the abject esthetic of their peers. Their schoolbooks wedged under their arms, holding each other's hands with fingers interlaced, they walked with slow, studied steps and the obvious desire not to be confused with the rest of the herd. The harmonious lines of their lithe, slender bodies could be seen clearly beneath the rough cloth of their stylishly cut smocks. Laughing and talking to each other in hushed voices, the girls passed in front of the terrace without deigning even to glance their way, despite Medhat's clever gesticulations to attract their attention.

"Did you see that?" cried Medhat when the girls had gone by. "Oh, if only that son of a bitch had been here!"

"Who on earth are you talking about?" Teymour inquired.

"Why, Imtaz, of course! He was supposed to meet me here."

"The actor Imtaz?"

"In the flesh."

"What's he doing here? I thought he was winning fame and fortune in the capital."

"Not at all. He came back to live among us almost three years ago."

"I find that very surprising. Do you know why he came back?"

"It seems there was a scandal of some sort, something that occurred on stage during a performance. I don't know exactly what it was all about."

Teymour remained thoughtful. This actor, Imtaz, although a few years older, had been part of their crowd for a little while before leaving for the capital, where he was destined for a stunning career. He was a wonderful fellow, with the beauty of a thoroughbred and a natural talent for acting. As a teenager Teymour had admired him wildly and had been very happy to learn about his success from the newspapers. He had long thought of him as the only person who had managed to escape the pernicious atmosphere of this city. Never would he have expected to see him return home, and now Medhat was telling him he had come back amid some murky scandal. So, even Imtaz's enterprise had failed; this homecoming, shameful and without fame, connected him to Teymour's own demise.

"I don't know why Imtaz's absence upsets you so much."

"But that's obvious," said Medhat. "Have you forgotten that he's a very famous actor? The magazines these young ladies buy were filled with his picture for years. He doesn't need to try to seduce them; all he needs to do his show his face. It saves us a terrific amount of time. Girls drop like flies when they see him. Listen; let me give you an example of his irresistible power over feminine hearts. Recently a movie in which he played a hunter lost in the desert was shown here. After several exploits, the hunter is bitten by a snake. Well, believe me, when that happened, loads of girls fainted in the theater. We had to call an ambulance."

"And you think you're going to sleep with those girls? Sheltered the way they must be, I can't believe you'd be able to corrupt them."

"Oh, don't you worry about that," Medhat said confidently. "They'll do whatever we want. I've only been on their trail for a short time. Today I was supposed to show them to Imtaz. The bastard promised to be here at noon. He must still be sleeping."

"But who are those girls?" Teymour wanted to know.

"Sisters. They belong to one of the best families in the city."

"So it's going to be even harder than I thought! Upper-class girls! They're practically untouchable!"

"You're behind the times. We're in the heart of modernism here. The daughters of upper-class families are the first to demand their emancipation. It was bound to happen. In every evolving society, social progress always begins with the liberation of women's asses. And since that's the only progress that will benefit us in any way, I have nothing against it."

Medhat was speaking in a serious voice, but it was to impress Teymour and to make him understand that his city was not inhabited by ignorant peasants. This arrogant young man had best accept, and the sooner the better, the reality of his situation and abandon his belief that love's base acts are solely the privilege of those living abroad. He scrutinized Teymour's face, trying to discern his reactions. But Teymour's face expressed neither surprise nor doubt; these stories of seduced girls, even if totally untrue, could only enchant him. And he had just been granted a comforting certainty: Medhat had remained as frivolous as in the past. What madness could have made him think, even for a moment, that Medhat was indulging in political conspiracies? He let out a quick laugh, as if at himself.

A timid sun had begun peeking through the clouds and now it flooded the square with a shimmering light beneath which the face of the peasant woman on her pedestal seemed older, distraught. Men crossed the terrace, going in and out of the café, giving the impression of carrying out superhuman tasks. Street sellers yoked to their carts appeared here and there on the square, singing—with the songs of prophets announcing the delights of paradise—the praises of their slim offerings. Their meager bustling was starting to spread.

"Do you have a place to take these girls?" Teymour asked.

"We have several," answered Medhat. "That's not the problem; the problem lies in being discreet. We are being watched. You have no idea what's going on in this city."

"So what *is* going on?"

"Believe it or not, people are disappearing!"

"What do you mean?"

"Listen to me. In the last few months, four people, most of them prominent citizens, have vanished from one day to the next without a trace. What do you think of that?"

41

"You're joking."

"On my honor, it's the truth. You can read about it yourself in the papers. Even the newspapers in the capital are talking about it."

"I'm stunned," Teymour admitted. "But what are the police doing about it?"

Medhat looked around to be sure no one was spying on them.

"The police," he whispered, "are completely out of their depth. They think these are political crimes."

"And that's why they're watching you?"

"They're watching everyone, but especially us."

"What makes them think you're involved in political activities?"

"Nothing. But how can I prove it? It's a complete melodrama. I wanted to warn you. We are all suspects."

"Even me? But I just got here!"

"You can bet they've already got their eye on you."

Teymour looked at his companion in astonishment, not knowing if he should be worried or ecstatic about this extraordinary mix-up. The idea that the police were so off track as to think Medhat might be a political agitator capable of assassinating government dignitaries was so inane as to be farcical. No doubt about it, Teymour's stay in this city promised to be full of delectable possibilities that he could never have foreseen. He burst out laughing and patted Medhat's shoulder as if his friend had just told him a very good joke. For an instant Medhat stared at him harshly; then, caught up in Teymour's contagious laughter, he too began to laugh.

Just then a shabbily dressed young man with a gaunt and woeful face appeared on the terrace, threading his way stealthily among the tables. Medhat abruptly broke off laughing and called to him:

"Hey, Rezk, come here! I want you to meet my friend Teymour."

The young man came over to them, bowed and extended his hand to Teymour hesitantly, as if he feared intruding on a reunion where he would not be welcome.

"I am honored," he said with an air of contrition, smiling ever so faintly.

"Have a cup of coffee with us," said Medhat. "I'm happy to see you."

"I'm terribly sorry," said the young man, "but I cannot stay. I must go. Excuse me."

He turned his head and made as if to go on his way, but Medhat grabbed his jacket sleeve and said, with misplaced intensity:

"Why don't you like us, Rezk, my brother?"

"I!" exclaimed Rezk, bringing his hand to his heart. "My word, how wrong you are. Believe me, I love you all."

"So, sit with us then. Just for cup of coffee. Please. Do me this favor."

For a few seconds Rezk seemed extremely discomfited; he grew even paler and his feverish eyes scanned the terrace as if looking for help. Then, with a resigned smiled, he grabbed a chair and sat down without saying a word.

"There, that's better," said Medhat. He called the waiter

and ordered a cup of coffee for the young man.

The new arrival's personality was of less interest to Teymour than the passionate tone Medhat had used to scold him for refusing to sit down with them. This was yet another mystery that Teymour was incapable of illuminating, and in fact more obscure than any he had encountered since leaving his father's house. This sickly young man in his threadbare suit was behaving like a frightened young girl; he didn't remember ever having met him; most likely he'd been a boy when Teymour left the country. Just what was his role in the crucial conspiracy that Medhat had cleverly mounted in this city in order to safeguard his pleasures?

Teymour waited calmly to see how the conversation would evolve. But the conversation was slow in picking up again.

The waiter brought the coffee and Rezk began to drink it in tiny sips, conscious of the gaze of the two men fastened on him. His face, with its delicate features slightly tensed as if he were suffering from some buried pain, was occasionally lit by a pale smile that invited sympathy. He seemed sincerely aggrieved by Medhat's suspicions regarding his good feelings for him.

"My friend Teymour," declared Medhat, "was away from our city for a long time. He was pursuing endless studies abroad. He's an immensely educated man."

"Pursuing studies," said Rezk in a dreamy tone, as if these grandiloquent words had struck a chord in him. "How marvelous! I am delighted you have returned among us."

"The honor is all mine," answered Teymour in a steady voice, without committing himself.

"You'll see him often now," Medhat said to the young man. "He won't be leaving us again. You were complaining about the lack of cultured men in our city; well, now you've got what you wanted. You'll be able to converse as much as you like with a superior mind."

"I'd never dare to bother him," said Rezk.

"You would not be bothering him," Medhat asserted. "Right, Teymour?"

"Not in the least," Teymour replied. "On the contrary, I'd be thrilled."

"It would be a signal favor for me," said Rezk. "In truth, I love to read. I suppose you must have brought back a pile of books by foreign writers?"

"Yes, a few," said Teymour. "I'd be happy to lend you some if you'd find it useful."

"Oh, I can't thank you enough! I am your humble servant. Here foreign books are like manna from heaven!"

"You see," said Medhat. "By insisting you keep us company, I only had your happiness in mind. Because I, Rezk, my brother, I love you."

Rezk had finished his coffee and was attempting to put an end to the dealings with his companions by means of silences, nods, and distraught glances toward the square. He was waiting for the moment to withdraw in a way that wouldn't seem rude.

Medhat noticed he was ill at ease and came to his rescue.

"You can go now if you want," he said, smiling.

Rezk sprang out of his chair like a robot unfolding its legs.

"Thank you for the coffee. I am very honored to have

45

met you," he said looking at Teymour intensely, as if he wanted to store his image on his retina forever.

As soon as Rezk had left, Teymour asked:

"What on earth was that? Where'd he come from?"

"He's a police informant," replied Medhat with sublime indifference.

: III :

WHENEVER HE LOOKED BACK on the episode, Imtaz
couldn't help reliving all the ghastliness of that moment
when, clasping his co-star in a fiery embrace, he had realized his error. He had stood there, stunned and filled with
absurd terror as he heard the audience shouting out sarcastic remarks, while his partner—the actress he was supposed to have taken in his arms—emitted the shrieks of a
woman dishonored before collapsing, unconscious, in an
armchair. Then the curtain came down, the catcalls and
the laughter grew fainter, and Imtaz tried to understand
how the catastrophe could have occurred. Over the course
of some hundred performances, he had played this scene,
in which he entered a living room where his fiancée and
her brother were waiting for him, by using as reference
points the spots where the other actors usually stood on the
stage. Despite his extreme nearsightedness, he was able to
distinguish the characters he had to deal with well enough
not to make any critical mistakes. At first he thought his
partners had exchanged places during the scene that pre-
ceded his entrance, and that his blunder had arisen from

this switch. But such was not the case. Nothing of the kind had occurred; it was almost as if he had deliberately chosen to head in the wrong direction. This realization led him to seek a psychological explanation for his behavior. Was it some unconscious drive that had sent him rushing toward his fiancée's brother? It seemed like the eruption of some long-repressed act—he despised the actress who played opposite him—she was a stupid, vulgar woman of about forty with sagging flesh who had, for a small fortune, been promoted to the ranks of celebrity by a wealthy merchant. Imtaz had a very hard time hiding his disgust whenever he acted with her. Each time he had to take her in his arms, she would latch on to him, hungrily seeking his mouth like a vampire thirsting for blood. It was therefore highly plausible that he had attempted to escape her adipose hugs and kisses by moving unconsciously toward her partner, a shy young man who represented absolutely no threat to him. This explanation restored Imtaz's confidence in his eyesight as well as in his sense of direction.

He was not, however, alone in studying the enigma of his strange behavior. The members of the audience who had been witness to his unfortunate embrace did not remain passive; they were quick to peddle all sorts of conflicting rumors regarding his morals and his origins. Some of them considered him a very reasonable man and praised him to the skies: these were the capital's confirmed homosexuals. They wrote him a long letter congratulating him for having finally made such a spectacular choice. The scandal died down rather quickly, but doubt lingered in people's minds. Imtaz's career as an actor was seriously compromised. Humiliated by this tragic mishap, he was forced to withdraw from the public eye: he no longer felt up to appearing on stage opposite actors who were becoming more and more invisible to him. One more gaffe like that, and he would be stoned to death. He would be cornered into revealing a secret no one knew, not even his closest friends.

His myopia, growing worse each year, was the bane of his acting career because Imtaz, not wanting to disappoint all those women who admired his tremendous good looks, refused to wear glasses. Wearing glasses on stage seemed unbefitting given the virile, womanizing roles that ordinarily fell to him. He did not even wear them in town, and so people took him to be haughty and distant, an attitude completely foreign to his nature. And indeed, his short-sightedness gave his gaze the impenetrable and secretive air that lay at the very heart of his legend. All his power over crowds—and especially over women—he owed to the perpetual dim surroundings in which he moved: human beings, with their indistinct outlines, seemed to have absolutely no influence over his fate. His indifference to the attentions of his enthusiastic public, to feminine smiles and glances—for the simple reason that he could not see them—made him appear to be a charismatic, disdainful idol convinced of his own flawlessness. Imtaz knew that his fame depended entirely on this imposture and he could not bring himself to destroy the myth he embodied by revealing his infirmity to the world. He was willing to do anything save spoil his beautiful face by donning a pair of ridiculous glasses. Rather than going around wearing such barbaric accoutrements—which would have explained the true meaning of his misstep on stage—he had preferred to disappear from view, and had chosen his home town as his place of refuge. He owned a modest apartment there; it had belonged to his parents, both of whom were now dead, and he had always held on to it because it was tied to memories of his childhood. He intended to wait there until the scandal was completely forgotten.

When he arrived back in the small city, he let it be understood by his old acquaintances that he had come to rest from the sheer exhaustion of the artist's life; people were happy to see him, and they did not ask for details, even though vague rumors of the scandal had reached the ears of the better informed. But Imtaz's alleged convalescence had already lasted three years and he no longer mentioned anything about returning to the capital.

He continued to act his part in the theater of the small city—a theater of vast proportions where no stage effects existed to rein in the bountiful spring of life, and where no curtain fell to bring the performance to an end. This play had roots everywhere; it proliferated in the city's every nook and cranny. Imtaz now found himself continually inspired; he was at once actor and audience in an infinity of intrigues that no playwright could have dreamed up. Each day a new role was offered to him in the flood of grotesque passions and spectacular trivialities to which his fellow citizens devoted themselves with proud tenacity. The absence of ovations and curtain calls was offset by a singular pleasure, that of enthralling real people and experiencing their love or their hatred with a living, vulnerable heart. He felt ennobled, and more triumphant than he had ever felt on stage.

The large mirror in its gilded frame that hung on his wall reflected nothing to Imtaz but a hazy face with blurry features, like the face of a drowned man floating in turbid waters. He stepped back slowly and all that remained was a pale patch of color, barely a faint glimmer in the misty distance. Among all the old family furniture that filled the apartment, this mirror represented for him an ever-present and persistent lure. Long ago, when his eyesight was still keen, he had often delighted in admiring the pure lines of this bronze mask and had entertained himself by changing its expressions at whim. What had become of this visage, and what transformations had it undergone over the years? He would never know. He was reduced to this dismal fate: being the only person unable to admire his own face. With an acute sense of frustration, he turned away from this vertiginous abyss that could only restore a tiny, unrecognizable portion of his own splendor to him.

The lure of the mirror was still menacing him when he heard the doorbell ring. He hesitated for a moment, then went to open the door.

"Peace be upon you!" cried Teymour.

Imtaz recognized the visitor by his voice and was relieved to welcome him without needing to lean forward to decipher his features. He rarely had such good fortune.

"What a wonderful surprise!" he said. "Please forgive me for receiving you in these clothes."

Teymour glanced at the loose silk dressing gown with its floral pattern in which Imtaz was cloaked, then bowed respectfully.

"Don't worry, you're impeccably dressed. It's you who must forgive me. But I needed to speak with someone. Something terrible is happening to me."

Imtaz took him calmly by the arm and led him into the reception room where the famous mirror had pride of place. When they were seated, Teymour pulled a newspaper from his pocket, unfolded it, and brandished it beneath the former actor's unfocused eyes.

"Here, look!"

"What?" asked Imtaz. "Another war?"

"No," replied Teymour. "Just another man who has disappeared in our city. But I knew this one."

Imtaz grabbed the paper, looked at it closely and pretended to be interested in the picture of a man dressed like a rich villager with a huge mustache, the tips of which curled up so high that they threatened at any moment to poke out his eyes. The picture had a black frame around it, as if the man were dead.

"How do you know him?"

"I met him at The Awakening, the day I went into town for the first time—I remember him because of his mustache. He really amazed me: he told me he was planning on living it up before going back home. He seemed like a rich man from a neighboring village quite smug about his wealth. When it came time to pay the waiter, he took out a wallet stuffed with bills and laid it ostentatiously on the table."

"Is that all you know about him? He didn't say anything else to you?"

"He said something completely ridiculous; he said that he envied me for living in this city."

"And where was he from?"

"From a village about forty kilometers from here. It says so in the paper. He was supposed to go home that same night, but he was never seen again."

"So. He was out for a good time," said Imtaz. "Well, at least the man was an optimist. Too bad he's been assassinated."

"According to Medhat, the police seem to believe these are political assassinations."

"That wouldn't surprise me. The police chief sees conspiracies against the government everywhere. It's his private nightmare. And we shouldn't complain about it."

"But he's watching us!" Teymour exclaimed.

"If he's looking for crimes, he won't find any, because we're not assassinating anyone. And while he's following this false scent, he's not paying attention to anything else. This business makes people terribly afraid; they shut themselves in as soon as night falls. And so do the police. Which works out perfectly for us for organizing our pleasures."

"I admit I'm somewhat curious about these mysterious disappearances," said Teymour thoughtfully.

"You're becoming quite interested in our little city," remarked Imtaz. "I'm very happy about that. I was afraid you'd need a long period of adjustment, full of suffering and bitterness."

He rose, took a few slow steps around the room, moving away from the mirror and then back again as if attracted by a magnet. He couldn't stay seated in conversation for long. His experience on stage forced him to strike various poses, and to shade each of his lines of dialogue differently.

"And what's going on with you?" he continued. "Weren't you supposed to start at the factory soon?"

"I've decided not to work for the time being," replied Teymour.

A few days earlier, Teymour had resolved not to accept the chemical engineering position he was being offered. The fear that he would be found out as a fraud had played no role in his decision; his forged diploma still seemed as valid as any other to him. He was motivated by a more disturbing feeling urging him to stay away from any steady occupation just as strange events were transpiring in the city—a vague but insidious feeling that chained him to the town's fate while demanding his complete freedom of movement and mind. He felt the need to pay as close attention as possible to the slightest vibrations that might occur around him. Ever since he had taken up again with the friends from his youth, things did not seem as simple as they had the day he arrived; appearances were beginning to crumble, little by little revealing to his astounded eyes flashes of an underground life somehow tied to his hopes for happiness. Old Teymour had no trouble accepting his son's strange ideas and did not attempt to comprehend why he refused to take up a high-level position, thereby losing all the advantages of his long years of study. In fact, his father liked things better this way, for at heart he despised all mercenary aspirations. The diploma, despite being tiny and austere, was sufficient to satisfy his paternal vanity. He jealously guarded it in a wardrobe in his bedroom, but never failed to exhibit it to his relatives and other visitors as if it were a museum piece that had cost a fortune.

Imtaz suddenly stood still, slid his hands into the pockets of his dressing gown, shot a glance at the mirror, then said:

"May I ask why?"

"I didn't study anything while I was abroad," Teymour stated. "My diploma is a fake that I bought right before I came home. I had to, for my father's sake."

"I see," said Imtaz. "I don't think you need to worry about that. We live in a world where everything is false."

"I know. And it wasn't my scruples that stopped me. A few days ago I was still willing to accept the job at the refinery. You can imagine that the prospect of living in this city after six years abroad seemed worse than death to me: what more could I have done for myself—better to be swallowed up by the daily grind and forget my misery—but now I have a feeling that I must remain totally available. It's as if I'm waiting for something. But what it is I'm waiting for, I cannot explain."

Teymour fell silent and looked at Imtaz as if he held the

key to all the mysteries that flourished in the city. But Imtaz was incapable of perceiving the question in Teymour's gaze; his myopia made him impervious to this kind of quiet desperation.

"I can't tell you how happy this makes me. I had thought for a moment that we were going to lose you."

"Lose me?"

"That diploma was somewhat of a challenge to my affection. I must confess that I expect nothing from someone with the mentality of a chemical engineer embarking on a career as a conscientious and responsible civil servant. That certainly would have come between us."

"You thought I had a real diploma," said Teymour with a hint of reproach in his voice.

"Forgive me. It wasn't very shrewd of me. I should have realized that a man such as you has no use for a diploma."

"A man such as I has nonetheless committed a serious error. I came back here. With a little courage, I could have managed otherwise. And my cowardice is costing me dearly."

Imtaz moved slowly, as if against his will, and returned to sit across from his guest. He hated playing the teacher, the most outmoded role of all. What he had to say to Teymour now was based on a simplistic idea, one that could seem insignificant and trite if he did not manage to infuse it with enough brotherly warmth to guarantee its true magnitude. Imtaz had no need to simulate this warmth; he felt it so violently that it burst forth from each of his words. From the moment he had seen Teymour again, Imtaz had been charmed by the young man he had known as a teenager and who wore the signs of his fleeting triumph in the reputed dives of the West with a kind of sad nobility. Now, his esteem and tenderness for Teymour had only increased, learning how casually he had bought himself a diploma, the way one buys a melon at the grocer's, thereby rejecting all the hallowed notions attached to this piece of paper. It was an important revelation, for it indicated a nature hungry for joy, far removed from any preconceived ambitions. Imtaz could see that Teymour was anxious and uncertain about the questionable future the city held in store for him, and he would have liked to cheer him up with his own optimism and affection.

"I am more sensitive than anyone to your distress," he said, "but I am sure you will get over it easily. Life is the same everywhere."

He pronounced these last words with difficulty, as if he were ashamed of proclaiming such an obvious truth.

"The same everywhere!" exclaimed Teymour. "How can you say that, Imtaz my brother! You have lived in the capital; you know very well that life there is completely different."

"There is no difference to a critical mind, for it can find sustenance for its joy everywhere."

"Even in this town! You've got to be joking."

"I'm talking about mankind. When you live among men, they will always offer you the spectacle of their sordid appetites and their idiocies. It's an incessant stage show, supremely pleasing to the lucid observer. And it is the same everywhere."

"But men's lives are not the same everywhere. And that, for me, is where all the difference lies."

"That's an illusion as well. You are still blinded by the ways of a boisterous, eclectic world. This is a small city. So the comedy takes place on a reduced scale and is played without pomp. You have to seek life below the surface—you can't stop at appearances. With patience and love, amazing things can be discovered."

"You're asking too much of me," said Teymour wearily. "I have neither patience nor love at the moment. I think the only thing left for me to do is to move to the countryside."

"What a nightmare!" cried Imtaz. "There's nothing gloomier than nature. You'll only lose your sense of humor in the country. Unable to criticize the trees, your intelligence will lose its edge as you contemplate the plowed fields, and then, it'll be very easy for you to sing the praises of your fellow men because you won't be here to see and listen to them. Don't make that mistake. You should never cut yourself off from mankind because, with distance, you're more likely to grant men extenuating circumstances. I love you too much to let you succumb to that weakness."

The afternoon was drawing to a close and the sky was growing darker through the windows, plunging the room into a hazy gloom from which the mute shapes of the furniture emerged. Imtaz could barely see anything around him. He felt as if he were sitting in a cemetery, alone among the tombstones, addressing his precepts to a ghost. Moving like a sleepwalker, he rose and flicked a switch; then he remained standing with his lovely profile defying the mirror in the distance, dazzled by the partial return of his eyesight and the clarity of the familiar outlines beneath the lamplight. This sudden light drew Teymour out of his dream of a bucolic escape. He gazed at Imtaz, eyes moist with gratitude, and said in a quiet voice filled with emotion:

"I know you're trying to help me, and I thank you for your concern."

"My concern," said Imtaz, "is in direct relation to my feelings of friendship for you. From now on you are part of the love and joy that governs our existence in this city. We would be in despair if we were to lose you."

"I am deeply touched. But I am afraid I won't be able to contribute much to your goal."

"And I am sure of the opposite. You'll see. Stop cursing this city; it has surprises in store for you."

"The first and most wondrous is your friendship! It's making me believe in other surprises."

"Come," said Imtaz, "I must get dressed now. I want to take you to Chawki's tonight. You've got to meet that man."

"That bastard!" Teymour protested.

"Bastards are the salt of the earth," Imtaz replied. "And Chawki is a genius of a bastard. Let us not deny this bunch the opportunity to entertain us."

Imtaz disappeared into his bedroom and came out ten minutes later dressed, as always, with discretion and elegance. He resembled one of those refined portraits of him that had appeared in theater magazines at the time of his notoriety. Walking toward Teymour, he held out to him an old gold pocketwatch, its delicately carved case inlaid with rubies, and said simply:

"Allow me to offer you this gift in friendship."

Teymour took the watch and looked at it with increasing wonder.

"It's much too valuable," he stammered. "I cannot accept it."

"Its value is mostly sentimental and that's why I'd like you to have it. It belonged to my deceased father. I'd like you to be his heir, just as I am. Aren't you my brother?"

"I don't know what to say," Teymour replied humbly.

"Don't say anything. Accept it, and you will make me happy. Come on, let's go now."

Trembling with emotion, Teymour slid the watch into his vest pocket, stared at Imtaz in silence, nodded as a sign that he had understood and then headed decisively toward the apartment door.

It was obvious that the city's residents had no intention of increasing the prestige of the evil sorcerer responsible for the disappearance of several prominent citizens by playing into his hands with nighttime strolls. As soon as dusk set in, they deserted the badly lit streets to shut themselves in at home and take stock, in the calm and security provided by locked doors, of the disasters occurring outside. The fact that until now all the victims had been rich did nothing to allay the fears of the poor. There was nothing to prove that, in the dim shadows, the infamous abductor had the ability to discern an individual's economic status before attacking him. Only the shopkeepers—a notoriously greedy race—dared leave their doors open during these nerve-racking hours; they felt that their merchandise provided them with a protective shield. From time to time one could see the smoking torches of a few street peddlers sleepily pushing their carts in anticipation of potential customers. The fleeting outline of the occasional passerby, either a reveler or a beggar, sometimes appeared, crossing the bleached zone of a streetlamp. In this lugubrious atmosphere, Teymour fell prey to wild thoughts. The mystery that hung over the city, these houses with their closed shutters, these soundless streets, these thick black clouds sweeping across the night sky all made him feel as if he were on the threshold of a strange and incomparable adventure. His companion's presence encouraged his phantasmagoric tendencies: Imtaz was advancing at Teymour's side holding him firmly by the arm; he seemed to communicate through this contact the warmth of his friendship, all the while guiding Teymour through the labyrinth of the night of fascinating horrors opening, infinite, before them.

Chawki's house was located along the river in the residential quarter. It was a large structure dreamed up by some anonymous architect, but haunted by the gigantism of the Pharaohs' edifices. It spread over four floors, its countless bedrooms—most of them unoccupied—furnished with bric-a-brac where opulence mingled with the worst mediocrity. Chawki had become master of the house after his father's death, and had changed absolutely nothing; his stinginess made him chary of any household expenditure. At fifty he was still a bachelor, and with his miserliness he had bullied several of his relatives, herding them together onto the upper floors; no one ever saw them or knew in just what various ways they were all related. He was generous only when it came to his pleasures of the flesh, on which he did not hesitate to squander fantastic sums. Everyone held him in contempt because of his base, lascivious nature and his offensive haughtiness, especially those poor families who were the unfortunate tenants of the myriad houses and hovels he owned in the city. These impecunious tenants often found themselves obliged to allow him to seduce their wives or daughters; otherwise they faced the dreadful threat of immediate eviction for not paying their overdue rent. Several times Chawki had been almost disemboweled by a husband or father made indignant by his conduct, but his elevated social and economic status had until now spared him from well-deserved punishment.

Chawki greeted the young men with the pomp and compliments he usually reserved for his future mistresses; he had pretensions to charm and easily persuaded himself that his unhappy victims were consenting.

"Welcome!" he cried. "What an honor it is for me to receive the elite of our younger generation!"

A contented smile played on his puffy face with its noticeably drooping features. He waddled about, rubbing his hands together, looking at his young guests in blissful admiration. Imtaz knew the fellow well and was very amused by his performance, but did not let on. With feigned dignity he introduced Teymour to their host.

"This is Teymour," he said. "I thought it was time for you to meet him."

"So this is the young man who has returned from

62

abroad!" exclaimed Chawki. "I am so pleased to see him. What a bountiful day for me!"

He led them down a long corridor that resembled a waiting room with benches and chairs lined up against the walls, then showed them into a spacious living area filled with leaden, pretentious furniture. Enormous chandeliers hung from the ceiling like stalactites, filling the room with a harsh light. The three men sat down around a low table with a bottle of whiskey, an ice bucket, and glasses on a tray. Chawki leaned in and began preparing the drinks. When he had finished, he offered glasses to his guests, then raised his own and said to Teymour:

"A toast to your auspicious return to our city!"

Teymour thanked him with a nod and brought his glass to his lips. He was watching with interest and perplexity the strange amiability of their host. Chawki's overly warm reception seemed to Teymour suffused with the desire to please, and he wondered why a man reputed for his wealth and his insolence needed to court their friendship.

Chawki had downed half his glass; he grazed his mustache with his fingertips, and, looking at Imtaz with anxious fervor, said:

"So, what news have you?"

"The news is rather alarming," said Imtaz with equanimity.

"Why is that?" asked Chawki, whose face had suddenly clouded over.

"It seems that the disappearances have begun again. I suppose you've read the papers."

"Yes, yes, I know all about it—a sinister affair. But we are here to enjoy ourselves among friends. What do we care about these disappearances? Let's talk instead about our business."

Never in the course of his cruel career had Chawki shown himself to be so flexible, so humble, as with this young man of lofty beauty who seemed always to look at him without seeing him, and who had found a way to torture him: for once his money was worthless. Detested by men of his own age and standing—who were married and living a decent life—Chawki had been parading around in proud solitude when he met the former actor. Enslaved by his own permanent state of arousal, he had noticed at once Imtaz's almost miraculous power over women, and had devoted himself to him body and soul in the hope of catching a few crumbs from the feast. Imtaz and his friends were the only people in the city who admitted having the same ideals he did; they seemed ever in search of erotic distractions. In addition, without spending a penny, they managed to seduce the kind of girls that Chawki, despite his fortune, had never succeeded in bedding. Spending time with these young men was an enthralling experience and it was becoming more and more indispensable to him. Even his miserliness had melted away: he was always ready to acquiesce to the wildest demands in order to have the right to participate in their games. Still, he was clever enough to realize they were making fun of him behind his back, and if he accepted without protest his position as ludicrous benefactor, it was for one simple reason. Chawki was tired of chasing after the impoverished female tenants of his miserable hovels, and he was hoping that, through the intervention of his young companions, he would be able to realize the debauched dream he had nourished for so long: to sleep with the daughter of an upper-class family reputed not to care about money. This desire, skillfully nurtured by Imtaz, was at the moment the great affair of his life. With the idea of playing a prank, Imtaz had promised to set up a secret meeting with one of those adorable schoolgirls from a good family who fired up Chawki's bestial sensuality with their innocent and modest air. Hoodwinked by this promise, Chawki was now entirely dependent on the former actor and, each time he saw him, never failed to inquire about the progress of this delicious plan.

Imtaz had understood perfectly what Chawki wanted to speak to him about but, with malicious pleasure, he pretended not to know and continued talking about the mysterious disappearances.

"We care a great deal," he said. "And do you know why, my dear Chawki?"

Chawki seemed taken aback by the question; his face assumed a comic expression of terror.

"No, on my honor, I do not."

"Because the police," Imtaz continued, "believe that my friends and I have something to do with these disappearances."

"What a ridiculous idea!"

"The ideas of the police are often ridiculous, but you can't blame them. It's their way of going about things. Don't forget that we are considered to be subversive minds here and, as a result, we are the first to be suspected as soon as some calamity strikes the city. Even if it's a flood we're talking about."

"A flood!" Chawki said, amazed. "That's astonishing!"

"Not at all. It's quite natural. The police could never carry out their task if they had no suspects. And we're here to guarantee them a modest yield. For the time being, it hardly bothers us. But we will be extremely upset the day you disappear."

"Me! Disappear! God forbid!"

"I certainly don't wish it on you. But you never know. After all, you are a very wealthy man and people know that you usually have a lot of money on you. If this itinerant criminal were to harm you in some way, we would no longer be mere suspects. Everyone in the city is aware of our relationship. They would think it was a long-premeditated trap."

"Are you serious?" Chawki asked incredulously.

"Of course," replied Imtaz, keeping his composure. "And I'll be grateful if you don't do anything foolish. For example, you would be wise to take all those rings off your fingers when you go out at night. They glitter so much that, from a distance, you could be mistaken for a city lit up to celebrate a national holiday."

"But I cannot take them off," Chawki declared, holding out his hands in a gesture of helplessness. "I've been wearing them for years; they're practically embedded in my flesh."

"That's a shame," said Imtaz with a pitying look. "An assassin will have no trouble taking them off you. Those people will stop at nothing. It's not hard work for them to cut off one, or even several of their victim's fingers."

Chawki shuddered, looking at his chubby fingers: bands of different widths, set with precious stones, shimmered beneath the light falling from the chandeliers. Seized by a hideous terror, he was trying to conceal it behind a jovial smile that grotesquely distended his mouth.

"What an awful joke," he said.

"It's no joke," Imtaz replied. "Remember that, from now on, our safety depends on yours."

Chawki turned toward Teymour and looked at him attentively, as if waiting for him to give his opinion on this shocking subject. All of a sudden he realized that Teymour had not yet taken part in the conversation, and he silently reproached himself for having neglected such a gallant visitor. He was impressed by Teymour's appearance and the style of his clothing imported from abroad. Clearly this young man was not just anyone; he had the face of an experienced carouser, and his arrival in the city would surely give new momentum to their little group of joyful companions. Chawki—controlling the panic that Imtaz's pernicious insinuations had just unleashed in him—resolved to change the subject, and directed the conversation toward less macabre small talk.

"Excuse me," he said to Teymour affably, in an almost fatherly tone of voice. "I have not yet asked you about your long stay abroad. Did it go well?"

"Exceedingly," Teymour answered.

"It must be a great change for you. Our city, alas, cannot withstand comparison to Western capitals. I mean, in the matter of pleasures."

"I had thought so until now. But I am in the process of

changing my mind."

Chawki's eyes grew wide, and his smile slowly faded, as if from intense surprise.

"Really!" he said. "That seems so unlikely!"

A silence ensued, during which Teymour observed the plump little man sitting in his armchair, his hands decked out with gleaming rings, his face a grimace beneath the weight of reflection. He was beginning to understand the interest that a figure like Chawki could arouse in a critical mind. The man's infamous nature was amply offset by his air of narrow-minded stupidity, which could easily revive a dying observer's optimism. In the painful monotony of the city, Chawki would certainly prove to be a comic element of phenomenal importance.

Chawki's prolonged astonishment led Imtaz to pursue his cynical strategy of bewitchment.

"My friend Teymour has fascinating ideas about how to put an end to the boredom in this city."

"Tell me what they are," said Chawki, fidgeting in his armchair.

"He doesn't want to talk about them yet. But you can trust him. As you can imagine, during his long stay abroad he developed an interest in every imaginable kind of pleasure. He knows ways to corrupt this city that will make it a place of debauchery known the world over."

As if dazzled by such a prospect, Chawki blinked several times before asking Teymour impatiently:

"What are you waiting for, my son?"

"For now, I'm getting the lay of the land," answered Teymour.

"And what is your impression?"

"The land's very promising. With a bit of perseverance, we'll manage to drag this city out of its drowsiness."

"May God keep you!" said Chawki with respect. "What a splendid idea your father had in sending you abroad!"

Pleased with his little witticism, Chawki regained his inane smile and leaned toward the table to refill his guests' empty glasses. The euphoria of the alcohol, combined with Teymour's wonderful intervention in the city's destiny, had made him forget Imtaz's warning about a bloody fate. What he did not forget were Imtaz's promises about the young girl from a good family, and he asked the former actor again how the affair was proceeding.

"I'm going forward, but carefully," answered Imtaz. "It's a long-term affair, as you can imagine. I am trying to plead your case with the person in question, telling her wonderful things about you. But I must act with a great deal of tact."

"You already have someone in mind!" cried Chawki. "Well, then, success is assured. You are a man of miracles!"

"By the way, we have arranged a party for tomorrow night," said Imtaz.

"Where?"

"At Salma's. I hope you have no objections."

"None at all," Chawki assured him. "Tomorrow morning I will have a case of whiskey delivered to her house."

Salma was a young woman from a poor family whom Chawki had seduced and abandoned but to whom he continued to give an allowance because she had been forced to leave home after she was dishonored. She lived by herself in an apartment where Chawki occasionally went to visit her. The young woman hated him passionately and only received Chawki in order to heap criticism and scorn on him. Imtaz was counting on this explosive situation to enliven the evening with some delightful battle scenes between Chawki and his former mistress.

"I see a surprise coming," Chawki resumed. "Is there some new development?"

"Yes," said Imtaz. "I will be bringing some very fine people with me. But I'm warning you, you must behave."

"Really!"

"It will be truly magnificent. Two girls the likes of which you've never seen before. A short while ago they were still at their mother's breast."

"I see," said Chawki. Then, after a moment, he added: "Perhaps I should send cakes. They'd like that, don't you think?"

Imtaz did not respond. He saw, as if in a nightmare, Chawki's smile spread across his face and then transform into a kind of horribly lecherous grimace. All of a sudden the cries of a child complaining of hunger and the sad voice of an old woman attempting to console him could be heard. The child's whimpers and the woman's voice seemed to be coming from some hidden recess of the house's upper floors. Chawki appeared not to hear them.

: IV :

AT THIS EARLY-MORNING HOUR, no one frequented the public garden save a few vagabonds still asleep on the lawn and a few miserable children come to scavenge for cigarette butts left the previous evening by night-time strollers. It was the only time of day when young Rezk was in an almost supernatural state of tranquility and solitude, when he could abandon himself to his favorite pastime. Sitting on one of the benches facing the river, he would diligently read a classical work by a foreign author whose language he barely understood. He read with difficulty, as if hypnotized, coming up against enormous problems of comprehension at every moment. When the meaning of certain terms remained completely obscure to him, he underlined them with the tip of his pencil: he would look them up later in a small dictionary he had obtained for this purpose. His thirst for knowledge could not be deterred by any obstacle because, with each sentence he managed to decipher, determining its precise significance, he experienced a fierce fulfillment, more exquisite than any sensual discovery. He read this book at the rate of a page a day, and he felt as if his mind had expanded extraordinarily since beginning this formidable enterprise.

There was nothing of the happy young man about Rezk; being part of this city weighed on him like a curse. Gentle and sensitive by nature, he would have liked to enjoy the company of young men like himself, and even form brotherly ties with the city's residents, but the hatred he felt for a single man checked his slightest impulse to friendship or kindness. He despised the hatred that kept his affection from blossoming as powerfully as he despised the man who was its object. It had been sheer chance that this hatred was born in him, to grow stronger over the years. Despicable acts were committed by the thousands in the world every day; why had he had to bear witness to one of them—the most abominable of all, because it was an affront to the dignity of the person whom he revered above all others? Rezk blamed fate more than human failings for the irruption of this hatred that was debasing his soul and making a cripple of him.

He had been fourteen when this wound that could never heal was opened in him. His father, an often unemployed worker, was a good man with weak lungs. He had managed to survive with his wife and two children by some kind of ever-renewed miracle. Chronic poverty had not demoralized or embittered him; on the contrary, he countered his bad luck with constant good spirits. Even in the worst wretchedness, he would find a way to cheer up his family with his witticisms and his indomitable sense of humor. Rezk adored him because in his company poverty took on a sort of joyous uncertainty, as if the next day one might wake up wealthy and thriving. Of course that never happened, but one felt such a reversal of fate were indeed possible. Their life could have gone on like this, without any remarkable occurrence, had it not been for his father's weakness for beautiful women and his compulsive need to seduce them at all costs. It was this obsession, inherent to his optimistic nature, that had wound up playing a dirty trick on him. At the time, the family was living in the basement of an ancient house located on a narrow, quiet street inhabited by shopkeepers and minor public officials in whose eyes they were no more than human wrecks. This third-tier bourgeois community acted offended by the behavior of this family of starving proletarians who, rather than spending their days whining about their misfortune, filled the alleyway with carefree laughter. But the contemptuous hostility of his neighbors barely made an impression on Rezk's father, who was above such concerns. Unaware of his unworthiness, he had spotted the young wife of a newly married civil servant on the third floor of the house across the way; she had a languid body and a disdainful expression, and Rezk's father had been trying for some time to win her over. One afternoon when he was alone in his house, seeing her leaning on her windowsill, he tried his luck yet again. Sticking his head through the bars of the tiny basement window, he began to pester her with impassioned looks as he whispered rapturous words about her voluptuous charms. The beauty seemed to appreciate these rather coarse advances, but nonetheless took great care not to display any immodesty by showing too obvious an interest. This romance had been going on for some minutes when suddenly the husband appeared at her side and, although not blessed with particularly good eyesight, quickly perceived the danger to which his honor was being exposed. The sudden arrival of this new character on the scene stopped Rezk's father's ardor in its tracks and he quickly pulled back but, to his mortification, his head remained caught. He made frantic attempts at extricating it, but he had to face facts: his head was stuck, irremediably welded to the window bars. So, with his usual good spirits, he gave in to his fate and stopped moving. He closed his eyes and patiently prepared to submit to the legitimate wrath of his adversary. The latter, exercising both his rights as a cuckold and his strategic advantage, revealed himself to be a master of the art of insults and threats; he felt all the more at ease since his victim was immobilized far below, and would remain for a long time within his range. He could, at his leisure, refine his curses and even dream up new ones as yet unheard in the neighborhood. This verbal avalanche brought out the alley's idle residents and was followed with enchantment by the local connoisseurs. All the while, no one thought to free the miserable womanizer who, like a martyr whose neck is shackled in irons, languished in disgrace. He was counting on his enemy's exhaustion, but in vain. Far from growing tired, his tormentor seemed on the contrary to grow ever more spiteful in his abuse. His voice became hoarse; several times he could be seen lifting the earthenware jug cooling on the window sill and taking a sip of water to relieve his thirst, like a politician who for a moment has run out of lies, haranguing his constituents. It was a great opportunity for him to show publicly that he knew how to defend his honor, and to discourage thereby all the single men lying longingly in wait to sleep with his wife. He could not be stopped. In fact the crowd was having too much fun to take the initiative to intervene in any way that would have put an end to the crazy dispute. The people remained attentive and joyful, they even began wondering about bringing out mounds of food in order to eat where they were; it seemed as though the performance would go on until nightfall. This is when Rezk, coming home from school, saw the gathering and then spotted his father with his head trapped between the window bars like a marionette in a puppet show dying a villain's death. At first he did not realize the scope of the catastrophe; he thought his father was playing some kind of game he had invented to dazzle the mob. But the silent distress signals emanating from the livid face sticking out of the basement window soon led him to grasp the tragedy of the situation. His father was not there to get a breath of fresh air; he had to be suffering from his uncomfortable position and he needed help. But what to do? To pull apart those cursed bars required incredible strength. Rezk was in despair over his helplessness and tears were welling up in his eyes when a man stepped out of the crowd, dressed like a rich city landlord, haughty and full of self-confidence. He walked toward the window then stopped in front of the torture victim's face, examined it closely, knitting his brows with something evil and nasty in his gaze. For a moment the alley fell completely silent; even the offended husband ceased his diatribes, as if someone—this man from a higher class—had taken over his role as dispenser of justice. Rezk held back his tears and waited anxiously for the result of this painstaking examination to which the newcomer seemed to attach exaggerated importance. He supposed the man to be no less than an engineer and imagined he was thinking about the best way to free the poor soul who had fallen into his own trap. Rezk was getting ready to help him with his spindly arms when suddenly the man leaned forward—no doubt to take better aim—and sent a fat stream of spittle onto his father's face; then he sniggered and left the scene, the delighted look of a sadist in his eyes. This man was Chawki.

Rezk had remained breathless and trembling before the awful gratuitousness of that spit. For an instant he was seized with the desire to run after Chawki and beat him to death, but he was still too young, too weak to tackle such infamy. He swallowed his anger to rush to the aid of his hapless father whose face, dripping with saliva, expressed an anguished surprise without the slightest trace of rage or fury. Over the next few days he kept this surprised expression, shaking his head often, like a man undergoing a cruel interrogation. It was as if he were attempting to grasp the mysterious reasons that had led a stranger to inflict such an insult. This effort seemed to take up all his time and energy; he refused to eat, would look at his wife and children in silence, and then start to rub his face energetically with a bit of rag as if a few drops of the fateful spittle were still stuck to it. He died a few weeks later, without having said a word, simply shaking his head one last time in a sign of total incomprehension.

Rezk closed his book and tucked it away in his jacket pocket, like someone indulging in a criminal act. He did not know why, but he felt some embarrassment at the idea of being caught educating himself in a foreign language. Looking around, he noticed that the garden was now completely deserted. The vagabonds, disturbed by the light of day, had abandoned it to go rest in more suitable places; as for the little cigarette-butt scavengers, once finished combing the paths, they went off about their business. Rezk shuddered; he suddenly felt very alone sitting in the damp wind coming off the river. With a feverish gesture, he wound his woolen scarf tightly around his neck and stood up. It was time for him to make his daily report to Hillali, the police chief. This degrading occupation was a constant reminder of his hatred for Chawki because it was to his father's premature death that Rezk owed this abasement and servitude. The poverty into which they had been driven then was nothing like what they had known in his father's lifetime, when good spirits and a carefree attitude had reigned supreme. Rezk had to leave school to take a job as a laborer in the factory, but his fragile health made him a very poor workman and after a short while he was laid off in a dangerously weakened state. It was his mother who had saved them from starvation by doing poorly paid housework for some of the city's middle-class families. The ups and downs of employment led her one day to the home of Hillali, the chief of police. Hillali was touched by her devotion to keeping his house, and he offered her his protection and advice. An upright man with an extremely generous heart, he had done more than just show an interest in the widow; he had also taken care of her children, especially Rezk, first by urging him to continue his studies, and then, a few years later, by providing him with the job of informant, an occupation that required no physical effort, but simply some contact with the city's intellectual rabble suspected of hatching conspiracies against the government. His gratitude to Hillali had forced the young man to play the stool pigeon, a role whose usefulness he seriously doubted; it seemed more and more like something his benefactor had invented to help him out. Indeed to this day he had not been able to uncover the slightest hint of a conspiracy. It even seemed as if the shady-looking young men whom he was assigned to keep an eye on, eavesdropping on them in public places, were completely unaware of the tyrannical powers that obsessed the police chief and against which they were supposedly rebelling. Rezk was now almost certain that all those young men were conspiring with just one goal in mind: to find a girl to make love to. But he did not dare say as much to Hillali, afraid of sullying the seriousness of his mission with such a frivolous piece of information.

Rezk walked along the boulevard planted with scrawny dwarf palms that stretched for about a hundred yards along the river. This boulevard, a decorative set piece, had cost the municipality a fortune. On one side it was lined with brightly colored detached houses that belonged to the city's elite. During the day one met hardly a soul: most of these mausoleums' residents led an idle and sedentary life.

Every now and then a servant shaking out a sheet or a rug could be seen through an open window, but that was all. As every morning, Rezk dreaded his interview with Hillali because he had no serious information in his possession, and so there was no haste in his step. He was thinking about what he had just read in the book by the foreign author, dead for two centuries, some of whose ideas stirred secret feelings in him. After having walked along half of the boulevard as slowly as a Sunday stroller, he turned into a dirt path on his right and strode with more determined steps toward the police chief's house. The official lived in a recently constructed apartment building that had pretensions to modernism; rather than balconies in the old style, each of the apartments had a glass-enclosed veranda. Rezk started up the clean and well-maintained marble staircase and climbed to the third floor, then rang the bell and waited, catching his breath.

The man who came to open the door was thin and flinty, about sixty years old, tall, clean-shaven, with closely cropped grey hair. He was wearing a severe navy blue wool suit, an embroidered vest with mother-of-pearl buttons, and black patent leather lace-up ankle boots. These clothes, with their outmoded appearance, gave his figure a quality of ascetic nobility that commanded respect. His gaze, tinged with a kind of haughty solemnity, contained a glimmer of benevolence when he recognized the young man.

"Greetings, Excellency!" said Rezk. He bowed, took Hillali's hand, and brought it to his lips in a gesture of filial devotion.

"Greetings, my son!"

Hillali closed the door and led the young man into his study, an unpretentious room with an almost administrative austerity. Even though he was tormented by the absence of any significant news to offer up for his employer's shrewd analysis, Rezk nonetheless had an agreeable sensation on entering this room; as every morning, his gaze was immediately drawn to the huge mahogany bookshelf with its rows of fat bound volumes; he was fascinated by their titles' clever brevity. The contents of this bookcase, which he never tired of contemplating, cast a magic spell on his mind and made these secret meetings, which his absurd occupation as stool pigeon imposed on him, somewhat less oppressive. The proximity of these books on law and sociology, subjects about which he hoped to learn more in the near future, increased his esteem for the police chief. For, despite what the mocking, slandering mob thought, Hillali was no fool. His learning, the scope of his knowledge, would have surprised all those of the city's residents who imagined, wrongly, that no provincial police chief could be of much value to his profession. They did not know that it was precisely such awareness of his own worth—along with his disdain for the baseness of the regime and those who sang its praises—that had gotten him relegated to this backwater. In truth, his arrogant attitude had made him not only lose favor in the government's upper echelons; he was also suspected of lending a willing ear to the unsavory opinions of the opposition. For this reason, he found himself obliged to be extremely vigilant in tracking down the subversive activities that had, over the last few months, taken a particularly fearsome turn in his own district. The recent rash of abductions of local notables placed him in an extremely dangerous position; the slightest lack of determination on his part could be interpreted as tacit complicity with the government's adversaries. Unfortunately he lacked any real proof of a conspiracy, or even anything that would allow him to identify its instigators, and so could not crack down on them. Having studied revolutionary terrorism in every shape and form, in every era, he was convinced these disappearances were linked to a political conspiracy; to attribute them to some common criminal was out of the question: criminals of that sort rarely run the risk of transporting and hiding a victim's corpse. In his opinion, only an organization obsessed with an ideal and dedicated to disorder was in a position to carry out such crimes. It was therefore only natural that his surveillance be directed toward certain citizens whose social behavior and anarchical opinions had long attracted the inquisitive attention of his detectives. The result of this strict surveillance was hardly encouraging; the people being watched used their excessive spare time to hide out and plot, far from the prying eyes of the police. Hillali knew they frequently got together at night, and that they often changed their meeting places, but he was still hesitant to intervene by arresting the most seditious among them. He was not at all sure that he had the situation under control.

He went to sit behind his desk, shuffled some papers, and waited for Rezk to take a seat in the armchair across from him. A single glance was enough for him to see that his young informant had nothing new to report. Nonetheless, he asked:

"Still no news about our chemical engineer?"

Rezk turned his gaze from the bookshelf, sniffled, rubbed his nose with a crooked finger, then smiled as if to excuse himself for his wandering attention.

"I'm awfully sorry, Excellency! He's a charming young man with perfect manners."

"I don't doubt it. But that's not what interests me. Have you spoken to him since the last time we met?"

"No, not yet. I've seen him wandering around in different parts of town. He seems terribly cheerful. For a while now he's been gong everywhere looking like a happy man."

"That's very helpful information. I suppose, then, that his projects are well underway. He came here on a mission. I'd like to know of what that mission consists. You haven't managed to find out anything?"

"Please forgive me, Excellency! But I have the feeling that his only mission is discovering ways to have a good time."

Hillali shrugged in a gesture of disdain for his protégé's deductive abilities. Rezk often annoyed him with his excessive naïveté, but Hillali refrained from using harsh words to express his irritation. Rezk's waif-like figure of a pariah, his sickly and tormented face stirred remorse and compassion in the older man. The boy was of his making; he thought he had loved him as a son, and what he had made of this son was nothing but a monstrous caricature of his concept of a child born of his blood. A lamentable failure.

"Have a good time!" Hillali said with bitter irony. "Don't

tell me that he crossed an ocean to come have a good time with us. That's absurd! I'm suspicious of young men who return from abroad; they bring with them a world of violence and hatred. Besides, I'm convinced that this Teymour is the bearer of new instructions for his comrades. Otherwise, why would he have come back?"

"He's supposed to get a very good job at the factory."

"Yet we know he has not even been to the factory. Instead, he spends his time with the blackest sheep in town. Can you explain that to me?"

"He spent years studying to get his diploma. I think he may be taking a vacation."

"Think again! He did more than study over there. He was gone for six years and he only needed three for the degree. What did he do the rest of the time? He obviously must have been interested in other things."

"He's a scholar. I'm sure he wanted to add to his knowledge by prolonging his studies."

"What's to say your scholar's not here to make bombs! Don't forget that he's a chemical engineer."

Rezk gave a start and stared at Hillali in panic and disbelief. He had observed Teymour, had even chatted with him; nothing in the appearance of this young man from a good family, with his meticulous and slightly aristocratic attire, could lead one to believe he was a maker of bombs. He remembered Teymour's manicured hands very clearly; not a single trace betrayed unclean work of any kind—that such hands could be used to fabricate devices of death and destruction was hardly thinkable. Once again, it seemed to Rezk that the chief of police was losing his way in a mass of erroneous deductions that had no bearing in reality. Reality was simpler; why, then, did Hillali insist on complicating it by introducing such diabolical assumptions? The authoritarian delusions in all that smacked of perversion.

"Bombs!" said Rezk. "On my honor, Excellency, I don't think he's the type."

"You're letting yourself be impressed by the fellow's refined manners," said Hillali with the patience of a teacher imparting a subtle psychological notion to his favorite student. "And that's your mistake. You should know that the characters we're interested in long ago ceased fitting any stereotype. In our day, famished and filthy revolutionaries scarcely exist—they, too, have climbed the social ladder. The more educated and elegant they are, the more they are to be feared."

"But making bombs! That still seems completely unbelievable to me."

"I understand your surprise. You think that in a little city like ours such things cannot occur. Well, you are wrong. I've studied the question. This business is very serious."

Rezk remained silent. The puerile and rudimentary nature of his benefactor's teachings about police methods and psychology amused him; he felt like a kid again, playing cops and robbers. Despite his knowledge and his vast experience, Hillali was no exception to the rule that doomed adults, as soon as they began competing with each other, to the ruses of children. It was as though the entire world—including the most cultivated people—were perpetuating the harmless battles of childhood in crueler and more gruesome guises. Rezk was so captivated by this strange continuity of human instincts that sometimes he let himself get caught up in the game. He was incapable of understanding how an adult of Hillali's standing could—after all Rezk's reports—still make such faulty assumptions about a conspiracy, and a nonexistent one at that.

As if trying to convince himself that he wasn't dreaming, Rezk asked:

"So, according to you, Excellency, this Teymour came here to build bombs?"

"That is a hypothesis we shall need to back up with proof," Hillali replied. "Monitoring this young man is therefore essential to the investigation of this affair. Watch to see if he's carrying anything, a large package for example, when he goes to visit his friends. You need materials to build bombs, and you can be sure he's not undertaking this task in the midst of his family."

"I'll do my best, Excellency," said Rezk softly, bowing his head to signal his perfect subordination.

He had given up discussing the matter. To try to explain to Hillali the reasons he doubted the clear-sightedness of his theory would only exacerbate the slow decomposition of his physical and moral being, gradually reducing him to nothing more than a wreck: these tedious meetings exhausted him. He did not attempt to pull himself out of the mire into which his brain was slipping; he let himself be swallowed up in it, his gaze fastened on the bookshelf, holding itself there hungrily as if it were a last refuge for his wavering thoughts. The sun's rays coming through the glass of the veranda like fragments of scattered joy shimmered across the long rows of books with their colorful bindings, instilling in him a feeling of intoxication and a certainty that there existed other secrets, other mysteries to be illuminated, more important than the dull and childish schemes in which men took pleasure.

Hillali saw Rezk curl up in the armchair, and the suffering on his face frightened him, as if in his own home he had just come upon the remains of a dead man whom he had tortured in the distant past. He felt his insides contract at the sight of the immeasurable distress on this face that could have seemed handsome were it not for the expression of hideous pain manifest on all the features, even the smile. Was it fever that was eating away at Rezk, or was it the awareness of the stain attached to the role he was playing at Hillali's orders? Hillali had never managed to create between them the mutual affection of a father and son living in harmony and light. Of course, for that he should have lavished words of tenderness on Rezk and not forced on him the foul teachings of his profession, implanting in his soul the horrid idea of a world peopled with assassins. It was too late now to force these bonds of kindness and intimacy; humble and uncomplaining, he had to admit that his dream of fatherhood had failed, and learn to cherish the bitterness he felt as if it were the gift of an ever-merciful fate. Once again, he was overcome by a feeling of pity that made a mockery of his hopes, and he realized that the emotion would distort his mask of rigid austerity. He grabbed the dark glasses lying on his desk and quickly hid the sorrow in his eyes behind their black opacity. Now he could look at the miserable specter in front of him without giving himself away, and feast on this presence that had become as necessary to his solitude as the slightest flutter of his ulcerated heart. It took him a while before he could steady his voice in order to ask, with a hint of worried tenderness in his words nonetheless:

"Tell me, are they kind to you?"

Rezk raised his head and saw with astonishment that Hillali's gaze had disappeared behind the dark glasses. Those two black spots, large and glinting, resembled the visual organs of some fantastic creature and seemed to emit a powerful and insidious cruelty; they hypnotized him momentarily. Then he sniffled, relaxed his arms and legs and grinned wanly at the somber carapace that housed the old man's eyes.

"Who, Excellency?"

"All those people you are watching. I don't want to see you fall into some kind of trap. Don't trust them; they can be very nasty."

"It's not like that. On the contrary, they are very good to me. Still, they seem to believe that I don't love them."

"But, in truth, you do love them, don't you?" asked Hillali in the tone of someone seeking to wrest the last words from a dying man.

Rezk nodded imperceptibly in a sign of agreement; then he closed his eyes in shame, as if confessing his sympathy for the city's seditious youth concealed some defect, some abject meaning difficult to explain. He expected a reprimand, but none came. The silence grew, and he had the impression that the chief of police had left the room, carrying his secret with him. He reopened his eyes, saw that his benevolent torturer had not moved, and in a pathetic voice he asked:

"Is there something wrong with that, Excellency?"

Hillali hesitated for a few seconds before answering.

"You may love them, my son! It will allow you to observe them more closely. We don't have anything personally against these people."

On reflection, the young man's love for the sworn enemies of the powers that Hillali was responsible for defending, far from thwarting his plans, filled him with an odd sense of relief. What a wonderful easing of his remorse! So, this is how Rezk had managed to overcome his horror of his mission—by dispensing his kindness to those very people whom his disloyalty would lead to the gallows or the dungeon. Such a precious gift was more than Hillali could have asked of fate; and even though he felt tragically excluded from this love, his heart basked in the warmth of its radiance.

"Well, you may go now. Is there anything you need?"

Rezk stood.

"No, thank you, Excellency!"

Hillali rose, came around his desk, and approached the young man; for a moment they remained silent, one next to the other, as if united by a precious and unbreakable bond.

"See you tomorrow. And may God keep you, my son!"

Rezk leaned forward to kiss Hillali's hand, and Hillali had the distinct impression that he carried out this ritual gesture with particular fervor, as if he had sensed Hillali's pain and wanted to give him yet another pledge of his affection. He thought that all was not lost, and his heart trembled with unexpected joy.

When Rezk went out onto the street, a winter sun, warm and gentle, was pouring down on the city, plating the façades of the houses with wide patches of yellow light. This magnificent luminosity had a calming effect on the young man; he felt himself come alive again. Now that his report to Hillali was finished, he had nothing to fear from the day's adventure; he could go wherever he wanted and even forget the role of informant he had taken on almost as a dilettante, without believing in it wholeheartedly. In his own eyes, his perfidy only truly began when, alone with the police chief, he was forced to inform him of everything he had seen and heard during his outings the previous day. The rest of the time, until the following day, he was capable of regaining his honor and taking the law into his own hands. Brooding over his hatred of Chawki, he began combing the city for him. He needed to fan this hatred by laying his eyes on his worst enemy: he felt goodness and love overwhelming him and he did not want to allow himself to fall under their spell, which would make him weak. He rejected peace and refused to pay its price, which was forgiving the insult. He would never forgive—he had to hate Chawki and, through him, the thousands like him who defiled the earth as cruelly as a plague; it gave his life meaning and bolstered his pride. After a time he realized his efforts were ridiculous: it was too early for Chawki to be out and about. This realization darkened his mood. Nonetheless, he continued to walk aimlessly, head bent, pained and distraught, like a drug addict suffering from withdrawal, urged on solely by the strength of his hatred.

Suddenly his face lit up and he smiled as though he had seen a long-awaited and much desired apparition. He had just recognized Teymour in the person walking about twenty yards in front of him wearing a turtleneck sweater beneath a sports jacket and beige gabardine trousers, very narrow and extremely modern in cut. Rezk only saw him from behind, but he identified him immediately because of his stylish attire, which was second to none. Teymour was ambling lazily in the sun, stopping from time to time to examine, with an ecstatic gaze, the slightest oddity on his path, like a traveler for whom all the attractions of a city are as yet unknown but who wants to grasp its hidden beauties. Rezk's first impulse was to go up to him and speak to him, but his natural shyness stopped him; he slowed his pace and began to follow him at a distance, in such a way that Teymour would not notice him. In doing so, he was in no way thinking of spying on him. It was something else that pulled him along in the young man's wake: the simple pleasure of seeing him move about in these alleyways broken up by sheets of sunlight, like an ethereal creature from a wonderfully pleasant dream.

Unaware of the police chief's speculations about him, Teymour was strolling with a clear conscience and a soul freed from the terrors that had assaulted him on his return to his native country. Incontestably, he was far from imagining that he was suspected of building bombs. Since his meeting with Imtaz, his thinking had undergone a marked change; he was now making fun of his own behavior during those first few days, and he retained of this short period the shame of a man recalling a humiliating incident of his teenage years. He couldn't get over the fact that he had been foolish enough to let himself be influenced by the city's hideous outward appearance, that he could have lacked imagination to such an extent. At the moment he was eager to forget his prestigious time abroad with its long trail of easy pleasures in order to devote himself as quickly as possible to the new mysteries lying in ambush for him in the shadow of these dilapidated walls. The sleepy alleys, the shops where no one rushed to enter, the houses with their closed shutters seemed to contain all the pleasures that would soon be his through daring and guile. He was delighted to imagine that young beautiful women, frustrated in their sexuality, were on the lookout behind these ever-closed shutters, dreaming of secret and divinely romantic embraces. He felt himself transform into a love burglar—breaking and entering intimacies reputed to be unassailable in order to extract their fiery riches. He was already attempting to locate the houses where he could carry out his burglaries when he perceived the whispering of female voices above him; he raised his head, hoping to catch a glimpse of the features of a face or the stealthy complicity of a glance, but just then a bicycle sped past and skimmed him, spun around and stopped suddenly, blocking his path.

Standing on the pedals and keeping her bicycle in a wobbly balance by swaying her hips ever so slightly like

a tightrope walker, the graceful outline of the young saltimbanque Teymour had seen one morning performing in
front of the café on the square appeared in the middle of
the alleyway. She was dressed in parade clothes; her face
was made up in shades of pinks and oranges and trembled
in the soft light of the sun.

"Ah! Here you are at last!" she said with childlike joy.

"Were you looking for me?" asked Teymour, somewhat
dumbfounded by this encounter.

"I've been looking for you for days," answered the girl;
her tone was reproachful and she had suddenly stopped
smiling. "So, you haven't left?"

"No, I haven't left," said Teymour. "What made you
think I was going to leave?"

"You seemed so sorry to be here that my heart took pity
on you."

"Was it that obvious?"

"As obvious as a train wreck," she said, laughing at the
extravagant image that Teymour's misery as he sat on the
café terrace had brought to mind. "I could tell that you despised this city and you were thinking of leaving it. So I
smiled to encourage you to stay. It wasn't much, but it was
all I could do."

"Believe me, it was a lot. Perhaps I only stayed because
of that smile."

She looked at him in astonishment and joy.

"How wonderful!" she cried. "I'm so happy!"

Suddenly she let herself go, placed a foot on the ground
and clapped her hands to show her pleasure; then she
leaned forward and rested her elbows on the handlebars,

as if she wanted to make herself comfortable to continue the conversation.

"My name is Felfel," she said. "My father is dead and I live with my mother and brother."

"And my name is Teymour. I was abroad for six years. I only came back three weeks ago."

"What were you doing over there?"

"I was studying. I have a diploma in chemical engineering."

She seemed not to understand what a diploma in chemical engineering was; she remained hesitant for a moment, looking at him with a kind of frightened respect, her eyelids darkened with eye shadow.

"This diploma, is it some of kind of talisman you wear to protect yourself?"

"Yes, something like that," said Teymour, smiling at such naïveté. "But I'm not wearing it."

"Well you should be. Everyone here has an evil eye, I'm warning you."

"Don't worry. It protects me even if I leave it at home."

She had a doubtful expression about the power of a talisman consigned to the bottom of a drawer in a faraway house and, as if to dispel her anxiety, she rang her bicycle bell several times. The strident sound echoed in the alley like a call to riot, but no one moved and the shutters above their heads remained closed.

"Was it beautiful where you come from?"

"Yes, very beautiful," said Teymour.

The girl sighed, seeming to feel sorry for herself.

"Oh, how I too would like to leave."

"Why? Aren't you happy in this town?"

She made a face that signified all the disgust and horror the city inspired in her.

"There is no one here to appreciate my work. They're nothing but a pack of peasants."

"The other day you seemed to have had a lot of success."

"Success with the rabble! What good is that? All those men are only interested in the charm of my young body, not in what I do. They think I'm not conscious of their lecherous leering. But I know what they want."

She laughed, shaking her head, as if none of that had any importance. Then, all of a sudden, she seemed to remember something and hit her forehead with her hand:

"I'm such a fool!"

She rummaged feverishly through a small canvas bag attached to the handlebars, pulled out a slightly wilted red rose, and handed it to Teymour saying:

"Here, this is for you."

Teymour took the rose, gently inhaled its scent, then said:

"It smells good. It's very kind of you to offer it to me."

"Poor thing, it's not very pretty any more. I've been saving it for you for a long time."

She looked at him for an instant, eyes laughing, as if she were happy about the emotion she was arousing in the young man's heart.

"I don't now how to express my gratitude," said Teymour. "May I kiss you?"

"Yes, on the forehead."

Teymour leaned in and brushed his lips on her forehead.

Felfel had lowered her eyes; she raised them toward Teymour but this time she was no longer smiling. Her gaze was serious, as if Teymour's kiss had just sealed a pact between them.

"We understand each other, don't we?"

"I have never in my life been so close to understanding," answered Teymour with a quiver in his voice.

"I have to go now," said the girl.

"Will we see each other again?" asked Teymour.

"Of course. I ride around the city several times each day! Bye!"

She hopped nimbly back on the seat, turned the pedals, and with lightning speed raced off toward the end of the alleyway.

Teymour continued walking; he still held the rose in his hand and breathed in its scent from time to time as if he wanted to recover, in the perfume of the faded flower, a trace of his emotions from meeting the girl.

As soon as he had seen the little saltimbanque perched on her bicycle making a beeline for Teymour and blocking his path, Rezk had hidden in a doorway and from there observed the entire scene with utter amazement. The sudden revelation of a relationship between Felfel, his young sister, and the dashing and distinguished engineer who had recently returned from abroad was an extremely anomalous event worthy of all his curiosity. The brazen nonchalance with which Felfel had approached the young man, and the equivocal appearance of their conversation, proved that there was, between these two beings so far apart in social status, an understanding and an intimacy that were, to say the least, bizarre. Was the chief of police right in thinking that the young man with the diploma had only returned to his home town to sow the seeds of revolutionary spirit among the people? For a moment, Rezk was tempted to believe it. But instantly this idea appeared ludicrous to him and he was ashamed of being so foolish. In any case, young Felfel could not feel wronged by an oppressive regime; illiterate like all her peers, she was not even aware that there was a government. On the other hand, she undeniably possessed nascent charms—which her saltimbanque's clothes showed in great detail—capable of igniting the concupiscence of a man of refined tastes lost in this town's putrefaction. And yet, strangely, the passionate nature of the affair between his sister and Teymour did not offend him at all; on the contrary, it thrilled him and brought to life an unforeseen hope: that of becoming close to Teymour and of being able to love him like a brother.

: V :

THE PHONOGRAPH WAS PLAYING a dance tune.

That evening, Salma felt strangely indifferent to the mood of the clandestine orgy pervading her living room. Wearing a green silk dress, her throat and arms laden with jewelry, her face glum beneath her makeup, she sat on the edge of the sofa staring at the couples swaying in front of her who were holding one another in voluptuous embraces disguised as dance moves. The music frustrated her and filled her with a kind of painful nostalgia for a bygone era. Mostly she was annoyed by the hysterical laughter and childish behavior of the two girls Imtaz had brought with him and who, with immoderate intensity in their frail innocence, were rushing headlong into debauchery. As usual, they were middle-school girls who had been recruited as they were leaving their school grounds, and who had been so captivated by Imtaz's fame and glory that they had forgotten any and all self-restraint. Following the former idol's insidious advice, they had slipped out of their parents' homes in the hope of spending a night in amusements totally inappropriate to their age—a night

97

that, in their imaginations, they anticipated as rich in depravity of all kinds. More than anything they were afraid of not being able to rise to the occasion, and in their minds kept stretching the boundaries of indecency acceptable in such circumstances. After a few drinks they had become completely shameless. Salma, though she did not admit it to herself, resented them with the hatred of the bitter female: almost twenty-three, she already considered herself an old maid. All the men who came to her home to amuse themselves held her in the kind of polite regard normally reserved for a madam in a brothel.

These men had absolutely no intention of courting her, or even of feeling sorry for her. Their friendship was based unquestionably on an unfailing attachment to her, and yet they remained impervious to her inner turmoil—as they in fact were to all manifestations of turmoil in the world—as if for them life consisted mainly of the pleasures miraculously retrieved from the nauseating swamp of this city. She couldn't hold it against them; she was even grateful they had chosen her house as the den of their secret orgies. Her dishonor was known throughout the city, and so no scandal was great enough to further harm her reputation. At bottom, she was glad of their presence, instinctively appreciating the sarcastic spirit that animated their slightest words and their excessive contempt for all the institutions and conventions established by men. At times they gave her the impression of having been sent by some extraterrestrial power to record the immeasurable stupidity and vileness of the creatures on this planet.

The young men organized these licentious gatherings

at her home with the meticulous resolve of strategists plotting the fall of an empire. They not only diverted her from her sad mood; they also—chiefly—gave her the wild satisfaction of taking her revenge against the man she abhorred. For Chawki, that miscreant who in the past had taken advantage of her virginal soul, almost always attended in his capacity as their slimy patron of concupiscence and arrogance. She could therefore ridicule him at her leisure, lashing out at him with scathing, sarcastic remarks in front of vigilant witnesses wise to all his vices. It was for these intoxicating moments that she dug herself deeper into the ditch where she had fallen and refused to forget the past; she wanted to forever remain a living remorse in the eyes of the infamous man who had seduced her with his promises and dishonored her by abandoning her. He would never be rid of her. She would stay in this city forever as a woman marked by shame, and this shame would be reflected on Chawki and his descendants until the end of time. This was her only consolation.

After her misadventure with Chawki, there had been other men who had claimed to be in love with her and had offered to marry her, but she had always fiercely refused them. Nothing was to disrupt her in her pursuit of revenge. Until now she had followed this line, without asking anything from fate other than to thwart her seducer. No doubt she would have continued along this path if Medhat—surely inspired by some evil genie—had not one day brought under her roof a young man named Samaraï, a veterinary student, who had suddenly discovered a reckless and immense passion for Salma that made one think that, besides his mother, he had never seen a woman in his life. That brute was now in Salma's living room, sprawled out in an armchair and, holding a glass of whisky tightly in his hand, drinking excessively like someone getting drunk in preparation for committing a desperate act.

The story of this Samaraï was simply outrageous. A veterinary student in the capital, he had only come to this town to claim a small inheritance an old aunt had left him. He had got his money—approximately a thousand pounds—and was about to leave when, realizing he still had plenty of time to catch his train, he went to sit at a café near the station. Fate was such that, at this same café at the neighboring table, Medhat was in the process of figuring out what hope he could reasonably have regarding the future of humanity. This hope was so paltry—not to say nonexistent—that he looked around him so as to be even more convinced of the fact. No doubt this young tourist's air of importance (all the tourists Medhat saw had this same expression of importance, as if taking the train bestowed on them a certificate of heroism) inspired him with the idea of leading him astray. So he began talking to the young student and, after an hour of eminently instructive conversation, he had managed to dissuade him from leaving until he, Medhat, had initiated him into the fantastic pleasures this city concealed. Samaraï—young, shy, not very sociable, and entirely caught up in his studies—had been unable to resist his tablemate's seductive words. A certain idea of the world, a strange simplicity, had just been revealed to him and he was stunned by it, for nothing had prepared him for such a realization. Without leaving him too much time to think, Medhat grabbed the young man's suitcase and dragged him toward the exploration of the promised delights. Samaraï followed effortlessly; it seemed that he had at last found the ideal brother of whom he had been dreaming since childhood. Medhat's pernicious philosophy and his implacable sense of humor had erased in one fell swoop the memory of all those years he'd spent studying for his degree. The more he listened to his companion, the more life seemed to be essentially pointless and, at the same time, extremely interesting. A skilled guide, Medhat took him to various places, making him notice all the oddly magnificent details that were set in the surrounding rot and that only the arrogance of a blind man would refuse to see. Samaraï was walking on air; he did not understand by what magic this repulsive town from which he had been in a hurry to escape had suddenly assumed the appearance of a city with many extraordinary and delightful facets. He simply nodded his head, giving up on illuminating such enigmas for fear of breaking the spell. Every now and then he would stop to hug Medhat and kiss him, calling him his savior and his brother. They were tired and slightly drunk when, late one night, they arrived at Salma's.

It was the first time Samaraï had entered the den of a courtesan, and the experience was lethal. The perfumed and highly erotic intimacy he discovered inside the home of this richly kept harlot so intensely awoke the virility that had been slumbering for so long, that he fell in love with the young woman like a brute, that is, like a primeval man barely emerged from his native forest, and he no longer wanted to leave the place unless he were kicked out by the police. At first Salma was flattered and amused by this crude passion and she allowed him to move in with her, thinking that the young man's ardor would last only as long as he stayed in the city; but she quickly regretted her generosity when she realized that this ardor, rather than diminishing, was instead on its way to becoming eternal. In sum, this impudent veterinarian turned out to belong to that sect of men who instantly start thinking about marriage the moment they have slept with a woman, whether she be one-eyed, hunch-backed, or paralytic. From noon to night he hounded her with his passion, begging her to follow him to the capital where his studies were waiting for him and where he swore he would marry her. Salma responded to his constant exhortations with insults, calling him a poor beggar unable to feed even a bastard dog, and wound up spitting in his face, thinking that by treating him so offensively she would make him sick of her and he would go back to his stinking capital. And indeed her actions would have put off a man of some dignity, but nothing seemed to offend the fundamentally easy-going nature of this wild man; it was as if Salma's rudeness merely strengthened his fantasies of matrimony. The situation had become intolerable for the young woman because, despite the affection she was beginning to have for her lover (his stubbornness and his coarse meddling in her private life had in the end made her vulnerable to his spirited professions of love), she did not want to abandon everything she had gained through her dishonor to face the unknown and its potential new setbacks. Yes, she was dishonored, but the sumptuous apartment and substantial monthly allowance Chawki gave her were major assets for gaining respect in the neighborhood. In truth, the myth of the fallen woman that she continued to keep alive only increased her respectability by injecting a whiff of tragic fatality into her situation, without which she would have been no more than a vulgar prostitute in the eyes of her neighbors. Samaraï, who was too unsophisticated to suspect his mistress of such dark ethical fraud, interpreted her reticence to accept his marriage proposal as monstrous harassment and, to console himself, had begun to drink. This diversion would have been inconsequential if alcohol (to which he was not accustomed) had not altered the usual sweetness of his nature and caused him to do things that horrified the people around him. He was on the verge of becoming a hateful character.

In the middle of the living room, the dancers were moving with a slowness that wholly contradicted the music's breakneck rhythm. Imtaz and Teymour, clearly performing a task that had no relationship to dancing, were holding the two young girls tightly in their arms, content to make them sway imperceptibly with movements slyly calculated to provoke and excite their sensuality. Suddenly the record stopped, but the couples continued to sway their hips lasciviously as if the music had been merely a long-forgotten pretext. When finally they drew apart, Imtaz dropped into the nearest armchair (the former actor did not dare venture out into the room where the furniture was constantly shifting) and took the elder of the damsels, whose name was Ziza, on his lap. The younger one, Boula, went to sit on some cushions piled up in a corner of the room, in the company of Teymour. Surprised at their own happiness and tipsy from the whiskey they had unsuspectingly imbibed, the young girls allowed themselves to be stroked and kissed, showing as much boldness as their partners in these preludes to lovemaking. One could tell they were prepared to do anything except return to their families, whom they were beginning to despise, even to loathe. This hatred of the conformity and ugliness of their middle-class surroundings had been instilled in them by Imtaz that very evening, during a short lesson that had made a decisive impression on their minds and served to hide their penchant for loose living behind a kind of revenge against their parents' imbecility.

Stretched out on the floor, leaning his elbow on a cushion, Medhat was as proud as a stage director who has managed to put on a show of international importance and daring for a provincial audience. He was thoroughly enjoying the thought of having proved to Teymour his ability to promote such refined pleasures in a city with a reputation for deadly boredom. This demonstration of his talents filled him with bliss and spared him from having to take part in the evening's delights. For a time, he had been vexed by the fact that Teymour had merely brought back a forged diploma from his stay abroad, as if by having a good time in those far-off lands rather than studying, Teymour had been making fun of him. But once this moment of wounded pride had passed, he was quick to pay homage to the willpower and the unyielding nature of his old friend; it was in fact quite remarkable that Teymour, having set foot in a trap of such magnitude, had managed to come out without a scratch and with all imaginable prestige. Full of admiration for this heroic deed, Medhat's feeling of friendship for Teymour returned more forcefully than ever.

Snuggled in Teymour's arms, young Boula suddenly began to laugh loudly at a rather lewd anecdote that her enterprising seducer had just whispered in her ear. She stopped after a moment and let out a long sigh of regret.

"What?" asked Teymour. "Are you sorry to have come?"

"Oh, no!" Boula answered. "I am simply sorry that my honorable father is not here to see me."

"Would you like me to go get him?" asked Medhat.

The girl opened her eyes wide, more astonished than frightened by this blunt suggestion.

"Would you be capable of doing such a thing?"

"Of course," said Medhat. "Your wish is my command."

"Well, go ahead then, show us how brave you are," said Boula with the perversity of a female ready to enjoy a good scandal.

"Watch out," said Salma. "He's quite capable of doing it, and a lot of other things of which you haven't the slightest idea. He's got the mind of a devil."

"You are extraordinary people," said Boula with touching sincerity. "I never would have believed that people like you existed in this city. How can it be! This party is the most wonderful thing that's ever happened to me!"

"And this is just the beginning," said Medhat. "We've got a surprise in store."

"A surprise!" exclaimed Ziza who, perched on Imtaz's knees, had turned around to address the others. "What is it? I want to know!"

"We're waiting for the funniest man in the city," answered Medhat.

"You'll see," said Imtaz, "he's got a very special sense of humor. You have to know him well in order to appreciate it."

"He's right," said Salma with a trace of bitter irony in her voice. "You really need to know him to laugh at him. Because on the outside he's a rather sinister individual."

"Well, you'll explain it to me," said Ziza, turning back to Imtaz and taking up her previous pose.

Since the beginning of the evening, Samaraï had not uttered a single word; he did nothing but drink and moan to himself, in the grip of his obsession. Sadly for him, he had discovered love and alcohol at the same time, and these two ingredients when mixed together had a disastrous effect on his nervous system. He was racking his brains to come up with a satisfactory solution to his dilemma. To break off with Salma and return to the capital alone was intolerable; he could not renounce his love. Yet the prospect of ruining his career by staying in this city filled him with remorse and fear for the future. He was a burly boy of twenty-four with thick features, a narrow forehead, and black, frizzy hair, all of which gave him the sorry appearance of a degenerate brute. Nonetheless, this virile ugliness was countered by eyes of steadfast sweetness that had a strange power of suggestion over animals. The way all the quadrupeds submitted to his handling, without struggle or protest, made him the envy of his veterinary school classmates. Unfortunately, this magne-tism had absolutely no effect on human beings, especially when it came to persuading a creature as intractable as his mistress. Accustomed to dealing with dogs, cats, and other domestic animals, Samaraï was surprisingly naïve in his relationships with women; before meeting Salma, he had not approached a single one. It could even be said that the thoughtless and vindictive nature of the female sex—despite being so widely disparaged—was completely unknown to him. And he had lost all hope of obtaining a reasonable explanation from the young woman because each time he vaguely hinted at something that questioned the legitimacy of her revenge against Chawki she grew fu-rious and took advantage of the occasion to mark him as her next victim.

Glass still in hand, he got up from his armchair and, with the zigzagging gait of a drunkard, went to squat on the carpet across from Medhat. It had just had occurred to him that Medhat—whom he thought of as his evil genie—owed him reparations of some sort, and that Medhat was, in this instance, the only agent who could intercede with his mistress on his behalf.

"Won't you speak to her?" he whispered, leaning in to-ward Medhat. "She'll listen to you."

"Speak to whom?" asked Medhat, staring at Samaraï with exasperation.

"To Salma. I cannot convince her to leave with me. Her stubbornness is making me lose precious time. My dear Medhat, you are the one who brought me here; it's up to you to get me out of here."

"You are unbelievable!" said Medhat. "Am I keeping you here? You can leave whenever you want."

"But I want to leave with her. And that's why I'm asking you. You are the man she admires most in this city. Talk to her; I'm sure you'll be able to persuade her."

Medhat was far from going along with Samaraï's wishes and he had absolutely no intention of undertaking the task of persuading Salma to leave with him. In addition to the fact that she provided them with a comfortable and safe haven, she was the best placed person in the city for arranging depraved trysts. He would have fought the entire world to preserve this priceless friendship from harm. The idea that Samaraï—for whom Medhat had expended all the treasures of his wisdom to shield him from the universal imposture—would try to take the young woman from them seemed to him the height of human ingratitude.

"My word," he said. "You are the most ungrateful person I know. What will you do in the capital?"

"I have to continue my studies," said Samaraï pitifully. "Time is passing and every day I realize I've begun to forget everything I learned."

"Oh, no!" said Medhat, almost with revulsion. "I don't care a whit about veterinarians. Anyone who tries to obtain a degree from such a corrupt society has a vile soul himself. To tell you the truth, my dear Samaraï, you disgust me. You really are beyond redemption."

"It's for her I have to study," Samaraï whined. "How can I possibly earn a living if I don't get my diploma? I love that woman and I'd like to save her."

"Save her from what, you imbecile!" cried Medhat, furious. "Who said she wants to be saved? She wouldn't leave the privileged spot she holds in this city and the kind of pleasure she finds playing her part as the seduced and dishonored girl for all the gold in the world. It's become her reason for living. With all your diplomas you will never be able to give her such a fine reason."

Samaraï was taken aback by Medhat's explanation.

"I don't understand what you mean," he confessed candidly. "You think she is happy!"

Salma was following with her eyes the young men's conversation from the sofa; and although she could not hear the words, she could easily divine the gist of the secret confab. She was aware of the danger hanging over the group because of Samaraï's intemperance, and when she saw him get up from his armchair and fling himself, reeling, into the room, she expected something reckless; her fear subsided, however, when she saw he had chosen Medhat as the confidant for his grievances; she had no doubt that Medhat, with his mischievousness and his sarcasm, would quickly reduce Samaraï to a harmless fly.

Suddenly Samaraï stood up, hesitated a moment, then headed toward the sofa where he sat down humbly next to the young woman.

"Don't you come near me, you son of a dog!" said Salma with repressed fury. "What are you up to this time, you monster!"

"You can insult me," answered Samaraï in the voice of a drunkard with intractable determination. "It will not stop me from killing that Chawki if he dares come here tonight. Then you will be freed from your vengeance and there will be nothing to hold you in this city any longer."

"You won't kill anyone, you poor, poor boy!" cried Salma. "Go live with your animals and leave the humans alone."

Either Samaraï's horrified expression put her in high spirits, or else she wanted to add crushing weight to her scorn, but suddenly Salma burst out laughing. For a moment Samaraï remained paralyzed by this laughter, as insulted as if someone had spat in his face: he looked like he had just been bitten by a poisonous animal. Then he stared at the young woman with a gaze filled with great indulgence, as if he were trying to ward off the evil spells contaminating his mistress' soul with this new glimmer of tenderness. Far from experiencing the beneficial effects of this gaze, however, Salma gave into her demons and continued to roar with laughter, exaggerating her frenzy so much that she writhed about and clapped her hands as if she were seeing something irresistibly comic. Imtaz and Teymour, who had stopped their lovemaking with the young girls, were waiting coolly for this demented laughter to come to an end. For his part, Medhat had sat up, ready to intervene; he was afraid of any confrontation that might spoil the evening in some foul way. Against all expectation, however, everything went off in a dignified manner. Samaraï abruptly left his spot, walked through the living room with the stateliness of a humiliated monarch, and disappeared into the bedroom, closing the door behind him. Salma immediately stopped laughing.

In the silence that followed, Teymour got up to start the record player again, and he and Boula began to dance once more.

It was then that a man appeared in the doorway, dressed in black and holding a cane with a chiseled silver knob in one hand and twirling his mustache with the other, smiling satanically. This was Chawki, eyes popping out of his head with lust who, using his own key to the apartment, had entered furtively in the hopes of surprising his friends in mid-orgy. He was cruelly disappointed by the austere atmosphere he found, for he had imagined that, by arriving at this late hour, he would at the very least see the young girls in a state of undress. Nonetheless, despite his disappointment, he retained his hypocritical smile and continued toward Salma to kiss her hand. Having performed this ritual, he greeted everyone else in turn, then went to sit next to the young woman, emphasizing with a conceited air his authority over the others. Then he began to stare at Boula's hips as she swayed in her partner's arms and he remained silent for a long spell; the contemplation of this phenomenon had made him mute and panic-stricken.

The physical perfection of those hips seemed to conceal all the obsessions of the universe and at last forced him to let out a sigh of distress.

"Forgive me for interrupting your conversation," he said to hide the turmoil of his senses. "Do go on, please. What were you talking about? Or perhaps it's none of my business?"

"On the contrary!" exclaimed Medhat. "We were waiting impatiently for you. We were wondering why humanity, after so many millennia, still remains as despicable as on the first day of its creation. We'd be curious to know your opinion."

Medhat stopped speaking and rubbed his hands together like a student who has just baffled his professor by
asking an inappropriate question.

Chawki reacted like a greenhorn. He had been expecting
a frivolous, even obscene conversation, and the idea that
these young people were talking about humanity seemed
a kind of betrayal. It was a hard blow to his intellect that
had gone soft from dissipation and become impervious to
any thought that was not sensual. Nonetheless, the most
basic politeness meant not quibbling about the choice of a
discussion topic, especially in a group of such importance.
He thought he could get away with simply spouting an idea
that was rather commonly held—that not everything in
man was so bad.

"But humanity isn't as horrible as all that," he said
with the conviction of a man who believes in progress and
civilization.

"What!" cried Medhat. "The proof of degeneracy is everywhere! Even a child can see it. I would be very pleased
to hear your arguments in favor of an idea so at odds with
the truth."

At this point in the discussion, Teymour realized that
dancing was no longer appropriate, and that other delights were in store. He went back to sit on the cushions
but, confident that this interlude would be more than
worthwhile, he stopped fooling around with his partner.
He was now concentrating all his attention on the out-
come of the ingenious trap Medhat had laid in the guise
of philosophical debate.

Chawki wished he didn't have to answer; the presence

of the two damsels whose youthful charms he was going over one by one in his mind deprived him of all power of reasoning. He hadn't come here to hold forth on humanity. Amazed that he was being forced to think at such a moment, he found the subject in very poor taste. But how could he make up for his gaffe? Even as he delivered his lame apologia, hopelessly ideological in character, and despite his foolhardy nature, he was hesitant to seem like one of the propagators of this considerably hackneyed falsehood.

"One cannot deny that humanity has progressed," he said without overly committing himself. "It is constantly evolving."

"Evolving in its instinct for lucre and plunder, I grant you," replied Medhat, bowing as if to emphasize his deference to his interlocutor's opinion. "But I'm speaking about spiritual progress. And in this matter I maintain that it has not progressed an inch."

To find himself in the shoes of a thinker was no easy task for Chawki; his only desire was to get out of them as quickly as possible. Smiling affably and pretending to take the conversation lightly, he asked:

"You're interested in humanity's moral evolution? My goodness; I would never have thought that of you!"

"You're wrong not to take our friend seriously," said Imtaz while stroking Ziza's breasts—he still held her on his lap. "His theory on the matter is quite original. He maintains that spiritual progress can only occur in a world of leisure. What do you think about that?"

"A world of leisure, truly!" Chawki exclaimed. "I don't understand. Please explain what you mean."

"It's quite simple," said Medhat. "From the beginning man's hardworking fate has made him unable to conceive of an ideal that is not material and does not correspond to his needs and his safety. All he thinks about is earning a living; this is what he is taught from childhood on. His only aim is to become cleverer and more of a bastard than everyone else. During his entire lifetime, he uses his ingenuity to provide food for himself and, once he has eaten his fill, to invent some sordid ambition for himself. When, then, does he have time to elevate his spirit and his mind? The tiniest thought along these lines is considered a criminal offense, immediately punishable by disapproval and starvation. Therefore, I venture to affirm that only people of leisure can attain a way of thinking that is truly civilized."

"But what's the solution, then?" Chawki inquired. "Humanity cannot remain idle; people need to work."

"Too bad for them," Medhat concluded. "That's their problem. I'm just stating a permanent truth that historians and thinkers have always dodged because it is simple and has little market value."

"I'd like to know," said Teymour, glancing conspiratorially at Medhat, "if this truth applies to everyone. Are there no exceptions?"

"Ah, there are exceptions!" sighed Chawki. He was now listening intently to every rejoinder; his instinct warned him that some stealthy threat aimed his way was creeping into the conversation.

"Obviously," answered Medhat. "Everyone is not sensitive to leisure in the same way."

"I think so, too," said Imtaz in his turn. "For example, the honorable Chawki, here present, has had leisure all his life; do you believe that this has improved him spiritually?"

"I cannot say," declared Medhat. "It is for the honorable Chawki to reveal to us in all conscience if he has managed to take advantage of his leisure."

"He's a scoundrel!" cried Salma. "I wonder why you are even talking about him. All the leisure in heaven couldn't change him; he'll forever remain a scoundrel!"

"Quiet, Salma!" Medhat intervened. "Let him speak."

Chawki was smiling inanely, twisting his moustache with a feverishness that revealed his unease. His fears were being borne out; one could not mention problems as explosive as the evolution of humanity without being splattered. He was long used to his former mistress's hateful words and was not especially offended by her shouts and insults; the danger was coming from elsewhere. How was he to answer Medhat's insidious question? He sensed that his pride was being attacked and he could not repress a sigh of fury.

"To tell the truth," he confessed, "I don't think I'm better than anyone else."

"Hypocrite!" shouted Salma. "You dare compare yourself to others? Listen, oh friends, to this vile man!"

"My dear Chawki," said Imtaz. "Your modesty does you credit. Nonetheless, allow us not to believe a word of what you say. You, no better than anyone else! Please! We all know the indulgence and fullness of your heart. You are man par excellence, a man whom this city perhaps does not deserve. Don't try to belittle your reputation, for it's the glory of us all."

Chawki's natural conceit obscured from him all the insolence and perfidy of this exaggerated panegyric. Unbelievably, he thought it would help soften the blow to Medhat's theory caused by his admission if he pointed out a shortcoming that his good faith would not allow him to leave undisclosed.

"I don't want to say anything against our friend Medhat's perceptiveness. In my case, however, his theory cannot be tested for I have not benefited from all the leisure time you have so generously bestowed on me. One mustn't forget that, despite my wealth, I am constrained by countless obligations."

"Oh, poor man!" moaned Salma. "He has obligations, the poor thing! I know your filthy obligations, you desecrator of innocence, you!"

Chawki turned to her and patted her on the arm.

"Come now, dear, why are you getting angry? This has been a most fascinating conversation and it's allowing me to admire these boys' intelligence. We are not here to be sad. Let's be happy. A bit of music will cheer us up; let's turn on the phonograph."

The young girls greeted these words, marked by a certain slavish restraint, with an immense burst of laughter; although they had not once penetrated the ambiguous meanings of this transcendent discussion, Chawki's frightened face and air of stoicism had amused them as much as a puppet show, if not more. Chawki, titillated by this girlish laughter, was keeping a rapt eye on them. He let his gaze wander over one, then the other, as if to encourage them in their mirth, swearing to himself that at the first opportunity he would demand certain liberties from them to which his social status, if not the nobility of his face, entitled him. In the meantime, he engaged in an affected little habit he had, which he imagined vastly increased the stateliness of his person and which consisted of breathing in through the nose several times, pinching his nostrils, and lifting his head haughtily. Alas, he had to stop this enormously persuasive exercise prematurely; a small detail that his eyes—fixed solely on the bait of the young girls—had missed until now had just produced a shock in his mind. Samaraï's absence, although in no way unusual, nonetheless caused Chawki to be assailed by disturbing thoughts. Had the veterinary student, disappointed by Salma's systematic rejection, returned to the capital alone? This was unwelcome news, destroying Chawki's hopes based on the young man's steadfast devotion. He had always considered Samaraï to be a gift from the gods; his arrival in this city and his unbridled passion for Salma were in effect a godsend, delighting Chawki in his miserliness. If Salma were to leave with her lover, Chawki would be spared the lavish monthly payments he made to the young woman and, at the same time, be released from any responsibility in her future misadventures; he would be rid of her forever. For some time now he had been hoping that this relationship would lead Salma to a clearer understanding of reality and of her future, but it seemed that a recent quarrel had separated the lovers. Why had that imbecile Samaraï given up so easily? It would be years before another crackpot of his kind would appear in this town. Chawki did not dare ask about the student because he did not want to show Salma that he had any interest in the matter; she already suspected him of finding something to his advantage in the situation. Suddenly he became glum and even Boula of the wondrous haunches seemed to be plotting against his purse strings.

Imtaz's myopia prevented him from noticing Chawki's flushed features; however, he could clearly make out the shimmering glow of the jewels that adorned his rings.

"I see, my dear Chawki, that you have not taken my advice. Believe me, it's worth bearing in mind."

"Ah!" said Chawki. "I'm sorry, but what advice is it you're talking about? I don't recall any advice."

"I asked you not to go out at night wearing all those rings that attract attention. Have you forgotten that criminals are prowling about our city? You can be sure that we will all be affected were we to lose you."

"I've told you," answered Chawki as if trying to excuse himself. "I cannot take them off; they're stuck to me like leeches."

He held out his hands, shaking his head with an expression of fatal powerlessness and, at the same time, he shuddered in hindsight at the idea that he had traveled through all those dark lanes risking death or kidnapping at every step. In truth, he had not even tried to remove his rings; they were the mainstay of his confidence and his haughtiness and, without them, he would have felt as ignored and naked as a beggar.

"What is most upsetting," said Medhat, "is that they take away the body. So we wouldn't even be able to attend your funeral. Oh, and while we're on the subject, I hear that the hired mourners, whose business is collapsing, have banded together to protest the incompetence of the police. But that's a mistake on their part; the police don't give a damn about the decline of our popular trades. However, I think that a notice addressed to our assassins requesting they return the bodies of those who have disappeared to their families would have excellent results."

"You could stick it in your newspaper," said Teymour.

"That's exactly what I plan on doing tomorrow," replied Medhat in all seriousness.

"Your cynicism delights me," said Chawki, smiling wanly. "Still, only a few people have disappeared. I don't think this can cause your mourners irreparable damage."

"You forget that the men who have disappeared have all been prominent citizens, and among the very richest. In such cases, these mourning mercenaries charge the highest prices. Any one of these funerals would have brought in more than those of a hundred poor wretches. So, you see, my mourners do have something to complain about."

"I feel sorry for those good women," said Chawki, who from time to time liked to show that he did not lack a sense of humor.

"Stop frightening me with your macabre conversation," interrupted Salma. "These stories are keeping me from sleeping at night. And those poor little ones," she said, pointing to the young girls. "You're going to make them die of fright."

"We have nothing to fear," said Ziza. "They only go after men."

"If they were attacking women," said Salma, shooting a poisonous glance at Chawki, "it wouldn't take me long to find the guilty party."

"What does that mean?" stammered Chawki, who seemed profoundly perturbed by the young woman's perfidious allusion.

"It means," Salma replied spitefully, "that it could only be you. How many women have you already murdered? And if they did not die, it was no thanks to you. In any event, it's as if they had."

Chawki raised his eyes to the ceiling and made a face to show he was too reasonable a man to respond to such illogical accusations.

Just then Imtaz, holding Ziza's head in the crook of his arm, began to speak to the young girl in such a way as not to be heard by the others.

"Now is the time to excite him. Go do your belly dance. You promised me."

"You really think I should?" asked Ziza, who was terror-stricken at her mission to excite Chawki. "What should I do if he tries to touch me?"

"Slap him," Imtaz responded coldly. "A good slap in the face, don't forget."

"Won't it cause a scandal? He looks like my father, you

know."

"So? They all look alike. As you get older, you'll see that all the bastards resemble one another, not only morally, but physically as well. And tonight's your lucky night because you'll be able to slap your father through a third party, with no fear of reprisal."

"Would it be all right if I did it another time? I've had too much to drink; I don't feel so great."

"I order you to do it immediately," said Imtaz caustically. "I don't like pretentious girls without nerve."

"Don't be angry," begged Ziza. "Just to please you, I'll be brave."

She immediately slid off Imtaz's lap and, with steady steps, walked over to the phonograph where she began looking for a record to suit her dance project. A moment later, the sounds of folk music could be heard in the room. The young girl positioned herself in front of Chawki, squatted down and, grabbing the fingers of her victim, pretended to admire his precious rings.

"What lovely rings!" she said in a tone of exaggerated rapture. "Where did you steal them from? I would be capable of anything to own ones like these."

From where he was sitting, Chawki could see Ziza's breasts through the neckline of her blouse, and he was pierced by a desire to stroke those globes of delicate flesh that seemed to be scoffing at him. Sensing that the entire group was watching the girl's audacious moves extremely attentively, however, he refrained from risking the slightest gesture.

He asked, playfully, as if merely in jest:

"And what *would* you be capable of doing, my precious soul?"

"To start, I'd do a belly dance for you," Ziza replied. "Open your eyes and watch."

Ziza swiftly stood up and, without taking her gaze from Chawki, withdrew to the center of the room where she stopped, her face suddenly very serious. Then, slowly, she spread her legs, arched her back, and stuck out her belly; with innate knowledge her entire body began to sway to the monotone and staccato rhythm of the music, following all the phrasings of a lustful dream. The members of the audience, silent and captivated for a moment, quickly shook off their astonishment and, to encourage her, started clapping their hands in time. This rowdy accompaniment seemed to stimulate the dancer's energy; the tremors she transmitted to her belly became longer and more frenzied, as if this part of her body, returned to its toil of the ages, were obeying an intimate violence independent of her will.

Chawki wanted to live forever so as never to have to take his eyes off this feast of flesh; but fate, ever blind, thwarted his wishes by a ludicrous incident. At the height of his excitement, he suddenly saw Samaraï appear in the living room. This revenant—whose sleep had no doubt been disturbed by the boisterousness of the group—was limping forward, and it was easy to see why: he was wearing only one shoe; he held the other shoe in his hand, brandishing it about like a makeshift weapon with a view to massacre.

Without explaining his bizarre behavior, he went directly to Chawki and said firmly:

"Curses on your mother! I'm going to kill you!"

The speed with which Chawki protected himself against the danger by covering his face with his arms accentuated the farcical side of this onslaught even more. Shaking with laughter, everyone in the room stayed where they were and none of them thought to help him. Luckily, the shoe Samaraï tossed at Chawki only hit him on the shoulder. Still, he let out the cry of a chicken having its throat slit, and fainted.

: VI :

TEYMOUR WAS WAITING FOR FELFEL in front of the
statue of The Awakening of the Nation. In her stylized
peasant dress the woman was still raising her arm to encourage a heedless people to revive but, as if responding
to her ludicrous call, against the metal railing that surrounded the monument, a vagrant was sleeping, snor-
ing shamelessly and thus undermining the morale of his
fellow citizens with his unfortunate conduct; whether by
coincidence or design, serious damage was being done to
the government's attempt—by means of this insomniac
and imperious peasant woman—to rouse the crowds from
their torpor. Teymour endorsed heart and soul the act
of this beggar, whose ostensible ignorance concealed an
age-old wisdom. The young man was now in a position to
appreciate the humor of such a spectacle, seeing in it the
expression of the lucidity of an entire people impervious
to the entreaties of a propaganda so obviously tenden-
tious. Not so long ago, the vagrant's attitude would have
insulted Teymour's intelligence and reinforced his bitterness; now it seemed the only legitimate reaction to the
attempt to reduce a people to slavery that lay behind the

esthetic of this modern sculpture. Denouncing its decadent symbolism by means of the most passive attitude of all—sleep—showed, he thought, a remarkable ferocity and was imbued with much more meaning than anything any rebellious intellectual, tangled up in his pronouncements, could have done or said against the system that had created the statue to serve its villainous cause. This revelation led him to have joyous confidence in the future and completely transformed his vision of things; already he no longer thought much about all those years spent abroad, and the memories he still retained of them no longer struck the same painful chords. As if trying to help him forget that period of his life, none of his acquaintances ever asked the slightest question about the countries in which he had resided, nor did they seem interested in what he might have done there. At first he found this odd conspiracy of silence somewhat distressing. He could not understand their reserve and thought it almost insulting. He had especially suffered from not being able to recount certain adventures to Medhat; his old friend showed himself to be particularly unreceptive to confidences of this sort, as if he found Teymour's long absence entirely negligible, nonexistent even. However, having searched and searched for the motives of such indifference, Teymour wound up suspecting that his friends were trying, by their tact, to help him forget a past that they sensed he still missed deep down. He was touched by this show of thoughtfulness, and had done his best to be worthy of their esteem by adapting as quickly as possible to his new existence and by erasing from his behavior and his appearance all traces that could have markedly set him apart from his surroundings. To this end, he'd given up his lavish clothing with its foreign cut and fabric that made him look like a sad-faced tourist roaming the catacombs.

The previous day, when they had met unexpectedly in the street, Felfel had arranged this rendezvous as if she were a breathless conspirator pursued by a pack of policemen; then she rode off on her bicycle like some mythical creature, without leaving him time to respond. The bold artlessness with which the girl had tried to hatch a love affair had greatly surprised Teymour and, at the same time, filled him with unanticipated happiness. He was impatient to learn just how this mysterious meeting with the young saltimbanque would unfold. Suddenly it seemed as if there were no superior places for love. Even in this dismal city, frozen in its gloomy austerity, hidden forces were at work to encourage desire. With genuine anxiety he looked in every corner of the square, hoping to see little Felfel's figure emerge as she sliced through the air on her bicycle. But the huge square was empty; he saw only a police officer of the most moronic kind walking at the speed of a grazing cow, half asleep with a sulky expression, for it was siesta time. As if drawn by a magnet, this policeman, lonely and starved for power, was heading straight for the statue. For a moment Teymour imagined he was going to interrogate it for some breach of the law, but in reality the policeman had it in for the poor beggar sleeping against the railing; no doubt he was jealous of the man's blessed fate.

The officer bent down, grabbed the man by the shoulders and shook him with that skillful sadism so characteristic of policemen carrying out their duties.

"Hey you, wake up!" he said. "You should be ashamed to be sleeping here, my man!

The vagabond turned his head, opened a bleary eye, and asked in a calm and distant voice:

"Why would I be ashamed?"

"What!" cried the officer indignantly. "Don't you realize you're sleeping beneath The Awakening of the Nation? Show a little respect, my man."

The dirty, wrinkled face of the man took on an expression of immense weariness, as if the officer's remonstrance were coming from infinitely far away and a superhuman effort were necessary for him to understand and react to it. He closed his eye and answered with morose seriousness:

"There's no rush. When you have woken up the entire nation, let me know. Why should I be the first?"

And he went back to sleep.

The officer gave vent to his rancor by spitting on the statue's pedestal, then walked away shaking his head as if he no longer understood the reasons for his presence on earth. His authority had been thwarted by a beggar's destitution and ignorance, and this incident—which occurred repeatedly—overwhelmed him with inexpressible despondency. A ghostly silhouette, he faded slowly, swept up by the dust that swirled across the square.

This surprising dialogue had the opposite effect on Teymour; it caused him to burst out laughing. For a moment this laughter was uncontrollable, as if he were drunk. Then he realized what bad manners it would be to disturb the noble sleeper with his boisterous, misplaced good spirits.

He suddenly stopped laughing and allowed his gaze to rest upon the man with brotherly affection.

At the risk of breaking her neck, Felfel was pedaling as fast as she could through the treacherous streets. With great skill she circumvented puddles, avoided potholes, and threaded her way among the horde of street children without slowing down or stopping. And sometimes, while she was performing these amazing feats, she would raise her head to admire a sliver of blue sky between the rooftops of houses with their crumbling façades; she found a resemblance between this sunny afternoon and the elation that gripped her heart—a young girl in love racing to her first date. For this exceptional occasion she had scrubbed her face and replaced her saltimbanque's outfit with a short cotton print skirt, an almost transparent yellow blouse, and white canvas shoes that had just been polished; the final touch to this elegant outfit was a slightly shabby leather bag slung across her shoulder that struck her on the side as she pedaled furiously. Dressed in this way, with her hair combed and braided, without a trace of makeup, she looked like a barely nubile little girl racing to school. Her desire to surprise Teymour had inspired her to carry out this magnificent metamorphosis— showing herself to him as wholesome, childish—the only thing that could in novelty rival the charming sophisticated creatures he had loved during his travels. She was counting on her youth to make him forget those distant conquests that his memory still cherished. Nonetheless, she remained vaguely fearful. In Teymour's prestigious person there was something of the inaccessible ideal that worried her; the young man seemed to have fallen from another planet. When she'd first seen him sitting on the café terrace and brooding, she'd understood that he did not belong in these abominable surroundings and that he was not going to drag out his exile here. She had smiled at him instinctively, as if trying to help him endure his misery, with the hope that he would recognize in her smile a sign of a complicity that united them in their shared horror of this city. She had believed she could buy time in this way—and save for later everything in her power to hold on to him through her tenderness and her love. When she had approached him the previous day on the street to set up the meeting to which she was now impatiently hastening, she had intended to confess her decision to belong to him without further delay. Teymour might leave the city from one moment to the next and she would have no warning; it was becoming urgent not to abandon him any longer to his depressing solitude. But what would happen if she had come too late, and, worse, if he were not interested in the love she had to offer? After all, she was only a child of the people, obliged in order to get by to perform this thankless job that was almost like begging. Yes, she was nothing put a poor beggar. She made a sad little pout at the sudden realization of her lowliness and began pedaling with increased ardor. The possibility that Teymour might rebuff her made her want to throw herself off a cliff and die.

So filled was her mind with the apprehension and joy of seeing Teymour again that, until the very last second, she did not see the obviously troubled man crossing the road deep in thought who was about to collide with her bicycle's front wheel. She braked just in time to avoid running him over, placed one foot on the ground, and was about to curse him when she saw that he was none other than her brother Rezk.

"So, this is how you crush the people!" said Rezk smiling as if he were delighted by this encounter.

"I'm sorry," said Felfel. "I didn't see you there."

"That's all right." Then, noticing Felfel's carefully chosen attire, he said:

"My word! You're dressed like a princess. Where are you rushing?"

"Nowhere in particular," the young girl answered; his question, and the mocking tone with which he showed his curiosity, unsettled her.

"Don't lie; I know everything." Rezk was still smiling and a glimmer of affection shone in his eyes, as if to give his words a sweet meaning of complicity.

"What do you know?"

"Oh, nothing," answered Rezk, patting her on the shoulder. "And don't you worry about a thing. I was only teasing you. Go on, get out of here and have fun."

Just as he was about to leave the young girl, he sensed someone watching them from across the street. He turned his head ever so slightly and was suddenly submerged by a wave of indignation that left him breathless. Hatred—a hatred that had the intensity of excruciating pain—made his limbs tense, clouded his eyes with tears, and covered his features with a livid mask. The man standing next to an orange seller's cart intently ogling Felfel's bare legs was the very man eating away at Rezk's insides. The gaze seeping from under his eyelids and expressing the most blatant lewdness belonged to the despised foe so long the object of his enmity; in rare moments of respite Rezk managed to forget him, the way one forgets one has an incurable illness. With the elegance of a provincial satyr, Chawki was leaning with one hand on his cane while with his other he was lasciviously twisting the end of his mustache. His lips were curled in a greedy pout and he looked as if he were debating with himself about the quality of the oranges, which the orange-seller was shamelessly comparing in a soft singsong to the breasts of prepubescent girls. But this transparent charade had not escaped Rezk, who shot a look at Chawki that stung like the point of a very sharp knife. Chawki felt the danger behind that look and seemed to make a quick decision; he glanced disdainfully at the oranges, then swaggered away, pounding the iron tip of his cane on the ground.

Felfel had not noticed Chawki's presence. She thought that the sudden distress she saw on her brother's face was an indication of some searing physical pain. She asked with emotion and tenderness:

"What's wrong? Do you feel ill?"

Rezk tried to control his anger so as not to alarm the young girl. He had never told Felfel about the contemptible incident that had occurred years ago and had caused his unflagging hatred for his father's tormenter. It was a secret he kept jealously to himself. Not a soul in this city was aware of this most awful, debilitating illness tearing at his flesh. He laughed a tiny, sardonic laugh, as if he were making fun of an inconsequential, fleeting pain.

"It's nothing," he said, with a quick, gentle caress to his sister's cheek. "Well, I'll be on my way. I'll see you at home later."

For a brief moment Felfel watched him cross the street with pity in her eyes; she felt remorse for having let him leave in this pained state. She had a fanatical and fierce love for her brother, strengthened by the complicity of an impoverished existence that led them to share the least morsel of bread, the slightest tidbit that fell from the sky. He was the sweetest, most understanding human being she knew, someone in whom she could confide wholeheartedly and to whom she had given all her adulation until Teymour had appeared on the café terrace, filling her with breathtaking hope.

As she shot out onto the wide deserted square, she saw him in the distance, standing in front of the statue with that magnificent casualness that somehow reflected his extreme scorn of the world, and her heart grew weak with worry. She attempted to pedal even more quickly, as forcefully as she could, as if she feared seeing him suddenly vanish, carried off by the breeze.

Having arrived in front of the young man, she braked sharply and looked at him with childish glee, as if she were filled with wonder at finding him still standing there, waiting for her.

"Climb on quick," she said breathlessly, pointing to the rear luggage rack.

Teymour smiled at her, incredulous; he was undecided

about the girl's invitation. He was hesitant to let himself be pulled along by her; it seemed as indecent as letting himself be carried by an old man. This was not the first time her behavior had surprised him but he decided that the situation was too amusing to turn down her offer. Laughing at himself, he straddled the luggage rack and, gently grasping the young girl's slender hips, he tried to lighten her load by tensing his limbs, knowing all the while it was futile. Felfel began to pedal again, but more slowly now; one felt that this extra burden weighed on the impetuous movements of her legs, reducing her usual virtuosity to nil. She rode through the square, passed close to the metal bridge, then turned sharply to the right, taking the road that ran above the river. Having appeared for a brief instant, the sun tucked itself behind a cloud and the air, imbued with the scent of the sea, suddenly took on a chill. Teymour, busy trying to keep his balance, hadn't yet exchanged a single word with his companion. Although the few pedestrians strolling along the road didn't seem the type to develop critical opinions, he was ashamed of his hardly glorious position and tried at first to hide his face behind his driver's back. Soon, however, he relaxed and allowed himself to be carried along in all tranquility; he had just rediscovered his old enthusiasm for this device with its light and supple machine-work that had been the joy of his teenage years.

Felfel stopped in front of the entrance to a public park and turned to Teymour to let him know the ride was over. They got off the bicycle and went to lean it against a tree, then followed a dirt path down to the riverbank. The young

girl was seeking the right place for intimacy and she led
Teymour to the foot of a dwarf date palm whose broad
leaves provided natural protection from the impudence of
voyeurs lying in wait behind the parapet of the high road.
They sat down in the grass and remained silent for a long
time, gazing at the muddy water of the river dotted with tiny
waves as it flowed into the nearby sea. In front of them, very
close to the opposite bank, a lone sailboat was making its
way with age-old laziness. Suddenly the sun reappeared,
lighting up the triangular sail with such uncommon bril-
liance that it looked like a magical bird. Felfel was bursting with tenderness, but she was also in awe of the young
man sitting next to her, indolent and nostalgic, like a rich
king for whom her humble offering was of no interest. Now
that she was alone with him, beneath the shelter of this date
palm whose wide leaves protected them from the intrusion
of the hostile world she despised, a feeling of reserve and
modesty prevented her from confessing all her love, and
her great fear of losing him. She could not know that, far
from being indifferent to her presence, Teymour was savoring with exquisite sensual delight the brand new emotions aroused by his adventure with the young girl. Because
she had freed him from the obligation of spouting the lies
that, since the beginning of time, were meant to serve as a
prelude to lovemaking, he was deeply grateful. He needed
no lies, no insidiousness in his approach to seduce this
young, primitive creature who had come to him without
wile or ruse. He forgave her ahead of time everything she
would do or say over the course of their short or long affair,

because she would never be the enemy of whom one had to be suspicious, but always the child who needed to be protected and loved in complete confidence. Reaching out his arm, he squeezed the young girl's shoulders, then leaned in and kissed her softly on the cheek. She did not move, but felt glad, full of secret joy.

"I'm happy to be here with you," he said.

Felfel did not answer. She was looking directly ahead of her, staring at the boat with its white sail, which was now beginning to resemble a motionless kite in the azure. Suddenly, without turning her head toward Teymour, she said in a voice as faint as a murmur:

"When are you leaving?"

The question disconcerted him and it took him some time to reply.

"Who told you I intended to leave?"

"I don't need to be told. I know you won't stay in this city for long."

"What makes you think that?"

"Because it's not a city for you. I'm sure you're dreaming of leaving here as quickly as possible."

"No, you're wrong. I've come back to stay."

"That's not true," said Felfel with the stubbornness of a little girl. "You're just saying that so I won't be hurt. But I have a premonition you'll be leaving soon. How can a guy like you be happy in such a hateful place!"

Teymour smiled at the young girl's obstinacy; he didn't understand where she had got the idea that he wanted to leave.

"I'm very happy, I swear."

"You'll leave; I knew that the first day I saw you on the café terrace. You looked like an orphan."

"You're right," said Teymour, laughing. "I cut a sorry figure. It was the first time I had been out and I wasn't yet used to the change." He stopped laughing and held the girl closer to him. "I was stupid. But that's over. I love this city and want to live here."

She turned and looked at him with a kind of commiseration mixed with anxiety, as if he had just said something totally absurd.

"I'm not lying," the young man said. "Listen, I'm going to tell you something that will prove it to you: I'm looking for a place to live."

"Why? Don't you want to live with your parents any more?"

"I need a place where I'll be freer. Somewhere we can see each other in peace. Do you understand? I'm even counting on you to find it for me. Look for something in the old city; it will be more discreet."

Felfel raised her face to him; it retained its doubtful expression. She seemed to regard this as an outrageous whim.

"What will you do? Are you going to work?"

"Oh, no! I won't do anything. We'll just love each other and have a good time. That's all I plan on doing."

"A man as educated as you cannot remain idle," said the young girl with childish gravity.

"You're mistaken," said Teymour jovially. "First of all, I'm not as educated as you think. My diploma, if you must know, is nothing more than a piece of paper."

He was pleased at the idea that he did not have a real diploma and that he ran no risk of ever working in the sugar refinery, or anywhere else for that matter. And he wondered to what he owed the keen insight that had allowed him to grasp the true meaning of life. Having landed among millions of slaves, by what good fortune had he come to be conscious of the possibility of escaping the common condition? It would have taken almost nothing for him to have fallen into the fatal trap laid out to men since the beginning of time by the bloodthirsty caste that got its power from imposture and deception. Only a miracle had saved him from this hell.

He shook his head as if to cast out a nightmare, then looked at the young girl staring at him uncomprehendingly, her eyes wide with surprise.

"You cannot understand," he continued. "But it doesn't matter; I'll explain it to you later. For now, try to find me a place to live."

"I'll start tomorrow," answered Felfel. "What kind of place are you looking for?"

"I trust your judgment. Let's just say something worthy of a saltimbanque."

"But you're not a saltimbanque."

"Yes I am; you just can't tell. You'll understand when you know me better. We are of the same race; that's why I love you."

"Do you know how to ride a bicycle?" asked Felfel, proud of her dexterity in this domain.

"I am the kind of performer who does not perform for

crowds. There are a few of us in this city."

"Here?"

"Yes. But don't tell anyone. We don't want to be recognized. People think we are dangerous conspirators, and we let them believe it because it amuses us."

Felfel did not attempt to shed light on the meaning of these puzzling words. It was as if she expected Teymour to express himself in a language that was mysterious and incomprehensible to her; this was in perfect keeping with the image she had formed of the young man. All she had retained of his words was the spontaneous confession of his love for her. That was enough to fill her with happiness.

Teymour took the young girl's face in his hands, contemplated it for a moment, then kissed her, this time on the mouth.

Felfel did not pull away. At this stage in the rite of love, her inexperience was obvious, but she was trying not to let it show by hanging on to Teymour's neck as if it were a life-preserver. When he released her, she laughed a little embarrassedly, then turned her head away and gazed again at the river.

A large rowboat was passing close to the bank, overflowing with several generations of a family. They were piled up in the craft—women, old men, children—like people fleeing a catastrophe, wolfing down all sorts of foodstuffs with the voracity of castaways. The boatman was rowing steadily and vigorously, like a precise and well-oiled machine, and seemed to be ferrying his pitiful cargo toward some infernal goal. Suddenly they all stopped eating and stared open-mouthed and frozen, scandalized by the intertwined couple seated on the grass.

"People are so vile," said Felfel, looking away from the craft. "I want to go far away so I never have to see them again."

At the sight of this unsavory and fraudulent representation of humanity, Teymour began to laugh.

"Do you think they are any less vile anywhere else? They're the same everywhere."

"That's not possible. Don't tell me they are that vile everywhere. I couldn't stand it."

"But it's the truth."

"So there is no hope," moaned Felfel.

"Why should that make you sad? Personally, I find them laughable."

"They don't make me laugh," the young girl declared. "They actually scare me."

She shivered with disgust, then seemed to remember something. Hesitantly, she picked up her bag from the grass and opened it. She took out a small square tin decorated with colored drawings, with a thin slit on one side: a piggybank. Then, lowering her eyes, she held it out to Teymour and said humbly:

"For you."

Teymour took the piggybank and shook it, listening. The chink of small silver coins could be heard inside. Felfel was suddenly ashamed; she did not dare raise her eyes to the young man.

"My word! You're rich!" quipped Teymour.

"Don't make fun of me. That's my life savings. I know it's nothing for you, but I'm giving it to you anyway."

Teymour raised her chin and made her look him in the eye. He was terribly moved by the girl's unexpected gift. What was it that made all of them want to give him things? First Imtaz had given him his dead father's watch, and now this poor girl was offering him this piggybank with all her savings inside. He felt his eyes filling with tears.

"Why are you giving this to me?"

"In case we go away together. I don't want to be a burden to you."

"But I don't need it. And in any case, we're not going anywhere."

"I would really be happy if you'd keep it."

"No, put it back in your bag," said Teymour, returning the piggybank to her. "Who knows. Maybe I'll ask you for it one day."

Felfel clapped her hands exuberantly; by saying that he might one day accept her money, Teymour had definitively become her accomplice. She threw her arms around the young man's neck and kissed him several times on the forehead and cheeks. Then she jumped up and said:

"I've got to go home. Can I drop you on the square?"

"I'd rather walk," answered Teymour.

They strolled up the path holding hands. Felfel seemed delighted by her afternoon. She went to get her bicycle, straddled it, then turned to smile at Teymour one last time as she pedaled away. Teymour watched her ride off until she disappeared at the bend of a lane. His heart was filled with emotion and he walked along the cliff road with the free and lively movements of a saltimbanque.

Imtaz walked around the terrace following an itinerary

familiar from long ago, without attempting to make out the vague figures seated at the various café tables. This was how he always proceeded when he was to meet someone, for his short-sightedness did not allow him to recognize in a single glance the person he was looking for. He risked making a blunder. Whereas, in this way, he gave the person who was waiting for him the chance to catch sight of him and call out. Not having been hailed by anyone, he realized he was the first to arrive and went to sit at a table on the outer edge of the terrace, his haughty and magnificent profile offered as bait to the passing women. A few moments later, a stout man with a shaved head and a mouth topped by a flowing moustache, eyes hidden behind dark glasses, came to sit discreetly at the table next to his. He took a tattered newspaper several months old out of his jacket pocket and as if his life depended on it pretended to be interested in the news. From time to time, without moving his head, he cast a sideways glance at the actor, then went back to skimming his moth-eaten paper. It must have been very painful for him to read the same news items over and over for his glum face expressed to those around him an enormous, unforgiving sorrow. Imtaz had no idea of his neighbor's little ruses. In the solitude of his murky vision, he was reviewing in his mind the details of a dirty trick he was about to play on Chawki, the fabulously wealthy landlord. Having given in to Chawki's repeated entreaties, he had finally promised to provide him the next evening with something to satisfy his most sexually stimulating fantasy: the young daughter of a good family, preferably a schoolgirl with ink-stained fingers, with whom to sleep. But this generous act was not

entirely without an ulterior motive; it entailed a grandiose practical joke that had been Medhat's idea. This idle,
inquisitive young man had discovered, among the new
recruits of Wataniya's brothel, a young whore just barely
fifteen who, scrubbed clean and dressed in a schoolgirl's
smock, would be able to make any certified sociologist believe she came from an honorable, even aristocratic, family.
Despite his miserliness, Chawki was capable of spending a
fortune when it came to paying the price of his sexual fol-
lies. No doubt he would shell out a huge sum to sleep with
this girl with ink-stained fingers doing her homework beneath the light of a lamp. Imtaz could already picture the
scene and was allowing himself to be mesmerized by the
work he was about to create, like a playwright developing
his characters under the influence of drugs. What particularly appealed to him about this prank was the fact that,
in addition to the wicked pleasures it concealed, it would
also bind Chawki even more tightly to their little group. By
seducing a minor, Chawki would be forever compromised
and could no longer refuse to participate in other base acts
with them. This was a goldmine from which precious nug-
gets could be carefully extracted without the slightest use
of blackmail. Of course, the blackmail would be tacit, a sort
of unsigned contract.

"Hi."

Imtaz raised his myopic eyes, recognized Teymour and
said simply:

"Sit down."

"Sorry I'm late," said Teymour as he took a seat.

"Don't be sorry. It was a pleasure for me to wait for you."

He could not discern the kind of jubilation Teymour's face betrayed, but the mere tone of his friend's voice allowed him to recognize the joyfulness and unassailable good humor that now filled the young man's appeased soul. Teymour felt freed for all time of those senseless regrets he had clung to when he first returned to this city. Imtaz was charmed by this change that he had, it's true, been expecting without real concern; he had never doubted Teymour's intelligence. The similarity of their fates made him consider Teymour to be another self. Hadn't they both gone down the same long road before returning to this desolate spot only to discover that, for them, no place on earth was desolate? The way the young man was beaming with radiant good spirits, Imtaz noticed with a shiver, was the undeniable proof that he had been totally cured and that from now on he had the ability to survive in this pitiable world.

"I am happy to see that you are adjusting so easily to life among us," said Imtaz, looking at Teymour with gentle warmth in his eyes that were, however, made vaguely pathetic by his nearsightedness.

"It's thanks to your friendship."

"Of which you are worthy. I knew it would be difficult for you to overcome certain prejudices that were preventing you from seeing an essential truth. But I never had reason to despair of your intelligence. Only an imbecile could be sad to be here, or anywhere else, for long."

Teymour bowed his head ever so slightly as if to thank

Imtaz for the great intelligence he imputed to him.

"I'd like to ask you a question," said Teymour. "Do you ever miss your work as an actor?"

"Not at all," answered Imtaz. "On the contrary; every day I congratulate myself for having abandoned everything. A job, any job, is enslavement."

"And fame?"

"To tell the truth, I had absolutely no ambition. You have to have a very vile spirit to hope for fame in such a moronic world. Display your talent or become famous for whose benefit? Can you tell me?"

"That's what I thought all those years I neglected my studies. I didn't understand why or for whom I was supposed to become a chemical engineer. It seemed so idiotic."

"We each followed a different path to wind up here in the end. Maybe that's a good thing. But look at Medhat. He was more far-sighted than either of us. I don't think he believed for one moment that he could find anywhere else a life more fascinating than the one he leads in this city. And that is why I respect him."

"I admit he surprised me. Do you know, he never asked me what I did during my long absence? I was gone for six years and when we met again for the first time he greeted me as if he had seen me the previous day. Can you explain his attitude to me?"

"He thought you had really finished your studies and that you had become a slave with a degree, infatuated with some ludicrous learning. In other words, someone not to be associated with. But at the same time, he could not forget your old friendship and did not want to upset you with insensitive allusions."

"You must be right. But now that he knows I have a fake diploma, he should trust me."

"I suppose he's afraid of making you nostalgic about that period of your life."

"I'm not. I don't have a single regret any more. I don't think of the past, but of the future awaiting me here with all of you."

"You don't have to convince me. I know it. I'd even go so far as to say that this certainty is essential for my own joy."

The man with the shaved head, all the while keeping his eyes on his paper, was leaning closer and closer to their table with the obvious intention of hearing a few snatches of their conversation. The little he had picked up seemed to have depressed him; these young men were engaged in philosophical considerations that went well beyond the scope of his role as secret agent. He could not with any decency draw up a report based on such nonsense. He leaned in a little more, hoping to grasp at least a few words revealing some germ of a conspiracy against the government, but he heard nothing; the alleged conspirators had stopped talking and seemed to be communicating through signs agreed on in advance. Frustrated and infuriated by this cowardly connivance, the man pushed his chest forward, listening for the least little whisper. He almost fell off his chair, caught himself, and began eagerly to read his paper again.

It was Teymour who saw the carriage drive up, the same one he had seen a month earlier that Wataniya used as publicity for her brothel. The same rachitic horse and the same sleepy driver on his seat led the antiquated vehicle jam-packed with chattering young girls exposing themselves in sequined dresses, cheap jewelry, and flashes of naked flesh. This time, the very young girl next to the driver was not offering herself up to the pleasures of an impromptu belly dance; she was sitting quietly on the lap of a person whom Teymour recognized at once as his friend Medhat. Medhat was in fact signaling his presence from afar, waving his hands erratically about as if he were inviting the people to thrill to his good fortune. When the carriage slowed down near the café, he extricated himself from the girl, patted her on the behind, then leapt to the ground with the lissomeness and arrogance of a post-coital cat. The carriage continued on its way, causing as it passed a few boos from the impecunious customers; the moment was decidedly not favorable to lewd outbursts.

Medhat sat down at his friends' table in great good spirits. He seemed a bit cocky about his performance and, not bothering with the usual greetings, he began to explore the terrace's resources with a practiced eye, seeking out some event worthy of his sarcastic remarks. He was not disappointed. Rather than an event, fate had bestowed upon him an ideal victim in the person of the policeman sitting behind them in his favorite pose—the diligent reader, recognizable by his ancient, decaying newspaper.

"Don't turn around," Medhat said through closed lips in a feigned dramatic tone. "There's a guy from the police watching us. We're going to have a good laugh."

The presence of a policeman in the vicinity had absolutely no effect on Imtaz's serenity; he was used to remaining calm and even to believing that everything brewing outside of his extremely limited field of vision was improbable. Nonetheless, in order to play along with the conspiracy Medhat was hatching for the benefit of the policeman, he asked:

"What does he look like?"

"I'll describe him to you some other time," answered Medhat in a skillful whisper befitting a worthier cause. "Listen, I've clinched the deal with Wataniya. She's agreed for tomorrow night. The girl will come to your house around 9:00. What time did you tell Chawki to come?

"At 10:00."

"Good. We'll have time to get the girl ready and teach him a lesson."

"She didn't ask to be paid in advance?" inquired Teymour, attempting to imitate Medhat's whisper.

"Yes, but I managed to work it out with her. We'll pay her tomorrow night, that is, with Chawki's money." Then, turning to Imtaz, he added: "How do you plan to proceed with that son of a bitch?"

"It's already arranged. I've led him to believe that the girl is too proud to take money from him directly. He is to give it to me and I'll take care of making her accept it as a gift from him."

"That should leave us with a nice little profit. Still, we are going to have some additional expenses. We need to buy some clothes and accessories."

"What clothes!" Teymour protested. "You're not going to buy that bastard a wedding suit!"

"The clothes aren't for him, they're for the girl," Medhat

explained. "We need to dress her like a schoolgirl from a good family. We'll take care of all that in a little while. In the meantime, let's give this ignoramus of a policeman the impression he's earning his keep."

"Why bother?" said Teymour. "He's not worth the trouble."

"I'm not mean-spirited," answered Medhat. "These lowly subordinates have to eat, too."

"Such generosity!" exclaimed Imtaz.

"It's not generosity. What would become of us without this bunch? Ridicule needs to be fueled."

Throughout the entire whispered conversation, the policeman was striving to maintain his pose as an anonymous and harmless individual, interested solely in world events. He gave the impression of posing for an amateur photographer of folk traditions. Medhat was not fooled by this stillness and watched him out of the corner of his eye; beneath his meek exterior, the man continued to give them his undivided attention. Suddenly he fidgeted on his chair, abandoned his reading, and took a sip of coffee, no doubt to jolt his brain numbed by so much concentrating. A moment later, he sighed, then looked at his watch and groused, seeming to indicate by this that only an important rendezvous was forcing him to languish in this miserable café. Ever the magnanimous one, Medhat realized that the policeman was becoming totally demoralized and some morsel had to be fed to him to lift his spirits.

Raising his voice just enough to be heard by the policeman, he said:

"It looks like that comet is heading toward us at dizzying speed and will collide with our planet in approximately one month."

"Why, it's the end of the world!" cried Teymour, who had grasped Medhat's cruel ruse.

"But not necessarily for everyone. The article in the paper maintains that only part of the earth will disintegrate on impact. There's a chance we will escape the cataclysm."

"I don't want to be a pessimist, but I have the distinct feeling that the catastrophe will occur here," predicted Teymour.

"If there is any justice in the world, it surely will," said Medhat. "Unfortunately, justice is blind."

"Still," interrupted Teymour, "it could be a false alarm. Newspaper articles are filled with lies."

"Not *The Progress*," Medhat asserted. "Those people are serious and highly qualified. They don't write lies."

The Progress was the name of the newspaper that for months the policeman had been using as a screen when he eavesdropped on the city's subversive elements. The imminent threat to the planet predicted in this very paper immediately began to torment him. He started to flip warily through its stained, yellowed pages as he sought the article in question. He soon gave up, however, looking quite distressed as he recalled that the news of the comet was in fact very recent. Should he buy a new paper? It would be a costly purchase and he would not be able to put it on his expenses. He closed his eyes to gather his thoughts, assuming that the young men would most certainly continue their discussion on this fascinating subject. After a moment it seemed to him that the murmur of their secret meeting was beginning to grow fainter and he opened his eyes just in time to see them leaving the café. Flustered by this hasty retreat, he looked at his watch, acting out one last time the charade of the missed rendezvous. Then he stood up and, from a distance, followed the young men who were heading nonchalantly toward one of the city's commercial streets.

: VII :

IN THE DESERTED STREETS, the night exuded an anguish that Chief of Police Hillali perceived without terror, as if the murder and violence that this anguish implied were tempered in his mind by a kindly, almost complicit curiosity about those determined men behind it all. It was with the vague hope of encountering these men and perhaps even falling into their pitiless hands that he had set out on this nighttime stroll through the city. He was haunted by the desire to know, to possess something tangible that would prove his insightfulness in this affair. His right hand resting on Rezk's shoulder, he walked like an old blind man escorted by his young guide, but this was nothing but a deceptive façade, for never had his gaze been more penetrating. Unfortunately, all he had seen since he had so impulsively begun this perilous stroll was the sinister and depressing spectacle of a city that had succumbed to lethargy and given itself over to the sleep of the dead. Those revolutionaries—kidnappers of notables—had managed by their evil exploits to usher an invisible, corrupting poison into his city, draining its substance. The calamitous atmosphere that now shrouded these unpeopled streets and

these dark façades with their tightly closed shutters struck
him like a desecration: it grieved him much more than the
fate of the few notables who had mysteriously disappeared.
He resented these men for having imposed not disorder
but total emptiness. Already when he had been sent to this
distant province by the authorities in retaliation for his
outspokenness, he had found the punishment too severe;
nonetheless he had resigned himself, hoping that the
tranquility and the easygoing pace of a low-key existence
would mitigate the drawbacks of his exile. He viewed it as
a kind of early retirement. He was pleased with the idea of
ending his days in these quaint surroundings, amidst an
unsophisticated people still unfamiliar with the various
protests shaking up the world. Ever since these mysterious
disappearances had begun, however, fear had plunged the
city into an unsettled mood, and driven him into the torments and doubts of an investigation that promised to be
explosive. Thus his acceptance of a mediocre but tolerant
and inoffensive universe had not been sufficient to pull
him out of fate's clutches. Trudging along with his hand
resting on his companion's shoulder, he gauged with nostalgia just how low he had fallen. He thought about his past
as if it belonged to someone who had no ties to him at all
and whose life story had been recounted to him by someone else. Images of streets sparkling with lights; cafés
with lively, amusing crowds; urbane gatherings appeared
suddenly in his mind as if they had been generated by the
ill-fated night's bitter rebuff. He recalled a marvelously
beautiful belly dancer who performed in a luxurious caba-
ret in the capital; she had been his mistress only for a short

time but she lingered in his memory with the power of a still-fierce passion. He thought she must be dead by now, or at least old and repulsive, and he immediately felt disgust and horror at his own old age. Alone, he was alone in this city, crushed beneath its malefic torpor; his only refuge was the affection he had for this sickly boy who was not even his son, and whom he had doomed to an ignominious job. Slowly he was yielding to disillusionment, as if these elusive revolutionaries, by the outlandishness of their crimes, were forcing him to acknowledge the absurdity of continuing an investigation aimed at their capture. He was not oblivious to the fact that tonight's stroll could end in disaster. The responsibility for kidnapping the chief of police would be claimed by those enemies of the state as a dazzling victory against oppression and would mean the definite end of his career. He was fully aware of this, but oddly unworried by such a prospect; he felt a kind of morbid desire—like a suicidal dizzy spell—to fall into the hands of those men who were risking so much in order to change the world.

Their motives were so familiar to him that he had no need to wonder about the aim of their subversive enterprise. It seemed obvious to him that their aim was to destroy the government and the established social order. He himself was not an unconditional supporter of that existing order and he remained ever sensitive to the seductiveness of rebellion. But he was there to defend this order and to foil his adversaries' conspiracies. His duty did not include despising those who placed their demand for justice above the honors and benefits of enslavement and, in his difficult investigation, he felt closer to the conspirators than to the powers he served. Without admitting it to himself, he respected in their acts a certain moral idea that had not been completely snuffed out in him—far from it. For never had he confused these men with the uneducated criminals and crude intrigues long noted in police files. The theorists behind this terrorism with its violent impact were of an entirely different caliber and were aiming well beyond some sordid interest in the money of their victims, whom they selected with diabolical shrewdness. Only educated and, above all, idle young men—leisure time was absolutely essential for honing one's critical faculties and elaborating an ideal—could sacrifice their time and future to this fight against iniquity; it was a painful struggle, constantly begun anew. Organizing these kidnappings one after the other without leaving a single trace or proof of their participation revealed an unrivalled expertise in the art of revolution. Hillali caught himself admiring this faultless technique and wondering through what magic they had learned such modern methods of political subversion. They had certainly not learned them in this city that had never, as far back as anyone could remember, had the slightest revolutionary leanings. But perhaps these things could not be learned; perhaps they were simply buried, like a precious gift, in the consciousness of certain beings destined to the noble task of denouncing the infamy of tyrants.

He looked up at the sky streaked with dark clouds behind which the moon made a few brief appearances, like the face of a woman at her window. Then he squeezed his

companion's shoulder, as if to remind him of the importance of their mission and to advise him not to let down his
guard. He had noticed that the young man had begun to
slip into a gloomy apathy, the result of his sickly state and
the severity of the cold.

Rezk took note of this discreet appeal to his attention
and asked in a respectful tone:

"What is it, Excellency?"

"Nothing, my son. I was just wondering if you were
cold?"

"Thank you, Excellency," answered Rezk, moved by the
old man's kindness toward him. "I feel just fine."

"We'll have to think about buying you a coat. You cannot go around dressed as you are now. The winter will be
harsh."

Rezk smiled sadly in the shadows. Unlike Hillali—
warmly wrapped in a roomy coat of black wool—he had
nothing to protect him from the cold, damp wind coming off the river except his usual woolen scarf tied casually around his neck. This wind felt like a sharp blade
perforating his lungs, but he refrained from uttering the
least complaint. Until now he had even abstained from
coughing so as not to disturb the police chief in his medi-
tation. The methodical slowness with which Hillali carried out his investigations, preferring the most destitute
neighborhoods, as if poverty necessarily hid traps of some
kind, seemed unproductive and pointless to Rezk. He had
a strong intuition that the old man took pleasure in awaiting danger and that his effort to apprehend the tragic
event in all its searing truth masked a more daring plan:

to serve as bait for a terrorist attack. This heroic and totally unexpected aspect of their venture made it even more insane. Was Hillali, motivated by some childish and imperious vanity, expecting to see those young men—whom his imagination had dubbed revolutionaries and whom he wrongly suspected of planning a widespread upheaval of some kind—suddenly appear? An illusion of this sort would surely lead them to catastrophe, for if ever they were attacked, it would be by ordinary criminals who thought only of robbing them and whose preoccupations were far from political. These shameless crooks would not differentiate between the chief of police and any other passerby with the appearance of a well-off bourgeois venturing into the streets at this late hour. Rezk was sure of this, but how could he admit his certainty to Hillali without offending him? Hillali persisted—through a phenomenon that defied analysis—in seeing in this whole business nothing but the perpetual plot against the government. It would never occur to him that no one in this city cared about the government and that some did not even know it existed.

Hillali withdrew his hand, numbed by the cold, from Rezk's shoulder and stuffed it in his coat pocket. Then he said, as if he were thinking aloud:

"Really, they are acting very strangely!"

"Who, Excellency?"

"What *are* you thinking about, my son? I'm talking about our young revolutionaries. Yesterday they bought a schoolgirl's smock in a notions shop. I learned this from one of my men who was following them. I confess I find it quite eccentric. A schoolgirl's smock! Can you tell me what on earth for?"

Rezk pondered the clean-shaven, ascetic profile, and he was saddened to realize how such a trifling matter could defeat the knowledge and intelligence reflected on this face. He smiled compassionately, then quickly repressed the smile, and answered in a mischievous tone quite unusual for him:

"No doubt they are preparing some prank. I know them; they spend their time having fun."

"You are mistaken. They pretend to be having fun, but it's a trick. In reality they are plotting against the government. Otherwise, why wouldn't they be working?"

"Maybe they find life more pleasant when they do nothing. It's a new philosophy. They've decided to put it into practice."

"These young men are educated," said Hillali. (He hesitated a moment, feeling that what he was about to say might present an attitude that would be, to all appearances, pessimistic for a police chief. Nonetheless he continued in the bitter tones of someone rather embarrassed to subscribe to his own opinion.) "They cannot remain idle without finding out that this world is abject and revolting."

"Why, Excellency?" asked Rezk, struck by this rather worrisome tenet. It seemed to him that something very fundamental was being touched upon.

"Because they have time to reflect," answered Hillali, with a hint of anger in his voice.

"As far as they are concerned, I think they must indeed

find this world abject and revolting, but they have no desire to change it. At least that's the impression they give me."

"Are you saying that they scorn this world too much to change it?"

"I'd say it's more indifference than scorn."

"So, according to you, what is it they hope for?"

"They're not hoping for anything. Life, Excellency, life alone interests them."

"It's not possible that they lack ambition to such an extent. One of them, from a very honorable family, has just come back from abroad where he studied for six years. You're not going to tell me that he wasted six years getting a degree if he had no ambition!"

"I think that even if at some point he had any, he's given it up now. His behavior is the opposite of an ambitious man's."

"How can you know that?"

"By the serene way he looks at the vilest things. There is love in his gaze."

"His gaze is what's most pernicious about him," Hillali affirmed. "It's the very gaze of rebellion!"

Rezk felt a joy mixed with remorse at the mention of the aristocratic student recently returned from abroad. His affection for Teymour and his friends was marred by guilt. These representatives of a strange sect were unstinting in their camaraderie and their human kindness, even toward him, the least of men. This had always surprised and frightened him a little, for he knew he was unworthy of their trust. Forgetting for a moment his lungs ravaged by the unhealthful night air, he thought longingly about those witty and carefree young men who possessed the magical gift of dodging all the constraints and taboos of a repugnant society that they seemed to find totally absurd. The information with which Hillali had just provided him—the purchase of a schoolgirl's smock the previous day—allowed him to catch a glimpse of some romantic, slightly scabrous adventure in which he would have liked to participate rather than having to deal with these insane forays into potential revolutionary intrigues. To be one of them and to share in their magnificent plans seemed the pinnacle of happiness. Unfortunately, he carried within himself the crime of a contemptible profession and it would have been dishonest to join their group without revealing his relation to the police. It was these scruples that had kept him from going to get the books Teymour had promised him, preferring to sacrifice his passion for reading rather than be accused of duplicity.

"Tell me," Hillali began again. "Have you ever seen girls with them?"

"Not that I recall. But that doesn't mean they're not sleeping with them. In fact, that's all they want to do. What other use would they have for a girl?

"You are too naïve, my son. You have no idea what's going on in the world. Girls today are just as dangerous as men. They are capable of doing terrible things. I'm sure they have a female accomplice."

"But why dress her like a schoolgirl?"

"No doubt to attract their next victim. No one is suspicious of a schoolgirl. She can carry a bomb in her schoolbag without arousing the slightest suspicion. The purchase of this smock is very serious; it points to a new operation ahead."

Rezk found this theory dazzlingly stupid. Still, he did not want to seem resolutely hostile to the police chief's reasoning, first out of deference to him, and then because he sympathized with the solitude of the old man mired in his faulty conclusions.

"It's quite possible," he said with conviction. "I'll do my best, Excellency, to find out who this girl is."

"Watch out for yourself. If they suspected what you're up to, they'd be capable of killing you. Act circumspectly. I would hold myself responsible if something were to happen to you."

Suddenly they heard the sound of footsteps and almost at the same time the figure of a man turning out of an alleyway appeared with the unreality of a ghost in the sliver of a streetlamp's light. Hillali and Rezk stood still, speechless. Walking some ten yards in front of them with the wavering gait of a drunkard who's had more than he can handle, the man seemed doomed to an ephemeral fate—a fleeting vision in the noiseless night. When he arrived beneath the streetlamp, he stopped and pulled from his pants pocket an object at which he glanced rapidly as if he simply wanted to reassure himself that it was still in his possession, then moved off into the distance, staggering toward an unlit zone. He reappeared a little farther away, in the pale light of another streetlamp, and began to look in every direction, wheeling around with panicky gestures as if seeking his way through a maze. He could be heard pouring out curses in a muffled voice, then softly singing the words of a sweetly moving popular tune. Still, he did not appear to be a beggar; rather, he was a young man dressed decently and even with some refinement. This was what alarmed Hillali, for it was this type of individual he expected to see loom out of the oppressive night: a revolutionary clothed in the showy rags of the bourgeoisie—the ultimate disguise in which to appear innocuous—ready to massacre the entire world. But this man was at odds with any system of belief. His uncanny, debilitating drunkenness placed him in the class of outcasts and implied a massive dose of desperation.

Rezk had recognized the young drunkard.

"Who is that?" asked Hillali. "Do you know him?"

"Yes," replied Rezk. "He's a young man who has been in the city for a few days. He's just come into an inheritance."

"What inheritance?"

"His aunt, who was from here, bequeathed him some money when she died. He's come to collect it."

"Is he planning on living here?"

"I don't think so. He's a veterinary student. He's studying in the capital. His name is Samaraï. I don't know anything else about him."

"A student. Is he in touch with the others?"

Rezk would have wanted to keep silent about Samaraï's relationship with the suspect group, but under the noble and inquisitive gaze of the police chief, he found it painful to lie.

"The city is small. They must have run into each other. I've seen them once or twice together."

"You never mentioned this Samaraï to me. Why?"

"I didn't see the point. He was supposed to return to the capital once he got his inheritance."

"So why didn't he leave?"

"Maybe he missed his train."

"You're talking nonsense, my son! Several trains leave for the capital every day. He stayed for a particular reason and one that I assume has to do with this business that's on our minds. I will at least have learned something about this individual during our stroll tonight."

Rezk did not know what more to say. In the end all this was becoming tedious. Once again Hillali was going back to his mania for relating everything to a plot against the government. Rezk knew about Samaraï's affair and consequently was aware of the ties that kept the veterinary student in the city. But this too-simple explanation would certainly have trouble penetrating the skeptical and suspicious mind of the police chief. So Rezk tried to find a more rational motive for Samaraï's prolonged stay in such an uninviting province.

"Maybe he hasn't got his inheritance yet? I've heard that some heirs wait for years for their money and often die in poverty."

"I don't believe it for a minute. This young man's behavior is shady to say the least. First he hangs around this city instead of going back to the capital and getting on with his studies. Then he spends his nights getting drunk and lurking about the streets as if he were protected from unpleasant encounters. Did you see the object he took out of his pocket? He looked at it anxiously, as if it were some dangerous thing he wanted to get rid of."

"In any case it wasn't a bomb," said Rezk without thinking. "It was too small to have been a bomb."

"How would you know? A carefully made bomb can be the size of a pinhead and still do a great deal of damage. There is nothing that proves that this veterinary student—and why did he choose this field, I wonder?—isn't carrying one in his pocket. I wouldn't be surprised if he were part of the plot. Follow him. And give me your report tomorrow."

"As you wish, Excellency."

"Try not to catch cold," said Hillali with a touch of fatherly affection, as if he felt remorse sending his companion to an almost certain death.

Samaraï was in an advanced state of drunkenness, but alcohol was only one act in his tragedy since the afternoon's break-up with Salma. This apparently definitive break-up, coming after a long series of arguments, had destroyed his vital reflexes, reducing him to nothing more than a human wreck devoid of any instinct for self-preservation. With no experience in the inconstancies of love and the suitable remedies for them, Samaraï was suffering from having been brutally wrenched from his sensual pleasures, like a fatally wounded animal unable to express its suffering except with squeals. His relations with Salma had suffered from a dismal lack of understanding since that momentous evening when he had caused a scandal by attacking Chawki, his mistress's protector, with his shoe. The assault, described as "stupid" by everyone in attendance, had disrupted a very pleasant gathering, and had also increased the implacable animosity Salma felt toward all men in general, and toward Samaraï in particular, as if he were now the prototype for the whole nasty crew. She no longer spoke to him except to respond to his slightest touch with curses, and seemed to fly into a rage as soon as she saw him in her vicinity. In reality, the young woman's reckless outbursts served to release the resentment that had built up in her since Chawki had abandoned her; since the notorious shoe incident that had almost put out one of his eyes, Chawki had not reappeared. Although he got off with only a slight lump on his temple, Chawki—with the excuse of a head injury that doomed him to an early death—had found the pretext to disentangle himself from his obligations to his mistress and to stop the allowance he had been paying since their amicable separation. The defection of her loathsome protector, apart from its financial implications, was intolerable to Salma's pride and had the disadvantage of depriving her of a vengeance perpetually fueled by new grievances; she felt robbed of the presence of a reliable enemy from a superior social class, and for whom she had a solid respect. And so she took out all her spiteful anger on poor Samaraï—a mediocre and insubstantial character in her personal tragedy—and used him as a pale substitute for the veritable object of her hatred. The worst was that she refused to sleep with Samaraï and he, with his primitive, unsubtle mind, grasping at the adage that a guest is due every consideration in the home of his host, became more passionate as he was confronted by the exemptions—which offended his sense of hospitality—from this rule. He had tried to drown his sorrow in alcohol while continuing to harass Salma and begging her to leave with him for the capital, describing it as a place of endless delights where they would be happy and fruitful. These tendentiously alluring descriptions of their future life together affected the young woman like those terrifying bedtime stories that prevent children from falling asleep. So that afternoon, while Samaraï was spouting his monstrous plans for their future, Salma spit all her scorn in his face, enjoining him to vanish from sight and go make love to one of those mangy beasts with which he had become acquainted through his studies. This last insult relating to his profession had oddly excited Samaraï, as if Salma's allusions to bestial love had awakened in his unconscious an unexplored form of eroticism. He had thrown himself at her to rape her, with all the ardor and clumsy weight of a bull toiling away for the preservation of the species. In the struggle that ensued, Salma defended herself like a virgin being attacked by an army of roughneck soldiers, screaming that her throat was being slit and shouting for the neighbors to come see the carnage. Dazed and defeated by this paroxysm of brazenness, Samaraï fled the house seething with furious thoughts and still trembling with unappeased desire. After walking aimlessly for a very long time, he regained some self-control and decided what any feeble-minded man who had been rejected by his female would have decided in such an instance. He would forget his frustrated passion by abandoning himself to a night of nonstop revelry in that sumptuous brothel inhabited by ravishing creatures about which Medhat had spoken to him when they first met in front of the train station. To calm his nerves that had been shattered by his mistress's murderous frenzy, he had begun his evening by drinking in various bars and cafés around the city while he awaited the auspicious hour for licentiousness. He always kept the money from his inheritance in his pocket; approximately a thousand pounds, it formed an easily transportable wad of bills. With such a sum he imagined he could pay an entire harem for an unlimited amount of time and this feudal dream, which had become obsolete in this miserable civilization, gave him a sense of power he had never before experienced. At the moment when Rezk and the police chief had seen him moving like a funambulist in the stagnant glow of a streetlamp, he had been looking for Wataniya's brothel, which could not be found under any sign. So he was walking along blindly, led only by his drunkard's instinct, hoping to meet someone who could point him toward this den of debauchery. It seemed, however, that even the stray dogs sensed the anguish contaminating the city and had decided to shut themselves in for the night.

He thought he was lost for good in this maze of alleyways haunted by bad omens when suddenly his drink-addled mind made out some slight chink in the silence, like the scurrying of a famished rat ferreting about in the trash. He immediately stopped moving and pricked up his ears, all the while seeking with his eyes this providential animal that, in his obsession, he imagined capable of giving him the brothel's address.

As Rezk continued to tail Samaraï, he had no preconceived ideas and certainly no intention of spying on him as if the man were carrying some miniature bomb. He had obeyed the police chief's order solely out of a sense of duty, and because he had detected in the veterinary student's odd behavior some terrible grief. At first, he had been puzzled by how easily this newcomer to the city had been admitted to the group Rezk admired; then, when he learned about his affair with Salma, he had begun to feel sorry for him: he was aware of the young woman's reputation as a despot. He was now certain that serious dissensions between the lovers had arisen, and Samaraï's deplorable state was enough to prove that these dissensions were more than a simple lovers' quarrel. Motivated by his natural kindness, Rezk had nothing in mind but to stay close to Samaraï and to come to his aid in the event that, were he to lose his faculties completely, he might need Rezk.

The faint glow from a nearby streetlamp lit Samaraï's face, accentuating his coarse features—he seemed exhausted, as if he were dying a slow death, and traces of tears remained. When he saw Rezk arrive, he looked stunned, then bowed to the ground in a grandiloquent salutation full of panache.

"Excuse me, brother," he said in a thick voice. "Can you tell me how to get to the house I'm looking for? I can't seem to find it."

"Of course," answered Rezk. "I would be happy to be of service to you."

Samaraï let out a sigh of relief and his eyes shone with mad hope, as if all his sorrows would finally end in joy.

"I'm looking for a brothel run by a woman named Wataniya. I've heard about it, but I've never been there."

"I know it," said Rezk. "It's the one with the most beautiful girls."

"Are there many?" asked Samaraï anxiously, as if the

number of girls was extremely important to him.

"I don't know exactly. There are at least ten."

"Ten, you say? Well, that will do. That's exactly what I need."

"But I must warn you, they cost a lot. It's the most expensive brothel in town."

"I don't care!" shouted Samaraï. "I'm ready to spend my entire fortune tonight. I shall sleep with every one of them, you can count on it. Because love is killing me."

He took the wad of bills from his pocket and, showing it to Rezk, said: "Look. I'm going to buy myself a good time that will make the earth tremble."

So, this was the object that had aroused Hillali's suspicion! Rezk was no less horrified by the sight of all that money than he would have been had it been an actual bomb. He looked at Samaraï's hand waving the wad in the dismal light of the streetlamp as if he were trying to tempt him, corrupt him, or simply provoke him. Did Samaraï take him for a thief and an assassin, and was he trying to get attacked so as to end it all? All this smacked of a suicide by proxy. Rezk was suddenly very afraid, as if Samaraï's exhibiting such a fortune in this sordid and deserted alleyway could cause lightning to strike them.

"Put that back in your pocket," he said gently. "I'll walk you to the brothel."

"I don't want to bother you," answered Samaraï, whose teary eyes were staring at Rezk with bizarre intensity, as if he had just recognized in him a long-vanished friend.

"It's no bother; it's on my way," lied Rezk with his usual kindness. "In fact, it's not far."

"Let's go, then," said Samaraï, speaking as if in a dream and stuffing the money back in his pocket. "I am grateful for the honor you do me."

"The honor is all mine," answered Rezk, grabbing Samaraï by the arm and pulling him along.

They started off, moving deeper into the opaque shadows, their two shapes merging into one in shared distress. Wataniya's brothel was not far from the spot where they had met, but in the tangle of alleyways it would have been impossible for Samaraï to find it without the help of someone who knew how to negotiate the anarchic ramshackle development so rife in this part of the city. Rezk had not let go of Samaraï's arm; he guided him, doing his best to adjust his own steps to the drunkard's spasmodic gait. The veterinary student walked with irritating slowness, almost letting himself be dragged by Rezk, as if he wanted to put off the moment of their separation as long as possible, as if he were hesitant to carry out his resolution to hurl himself into licentiousness and debauchery now that the time was near. But Rezk could not have guessed this and, for his part, he was eager, without seeming discourteous, to free himself of this companion and his importunate riches that jeopardized their safety. He gestured nervously to make Samaraï pick up his pace, and immediately regretted this petty impulse so contrary to his desire for friendship. Samaraï shot him a glance full of inexpressible surprise, seeming not to recognize in Rezk the charitable soul who had come to his rescue earlier, then shook his head uncomprehendingly and let himself be led on obediently, with a kind of painful humility. A few minutes later, they found themselves in front of an old house with barred windows where no light filtered through; a lamp hung over the door, which was painted a bright red. The light coming from this single lamp emphasized the house's isolation; it was surrounded on both sides by empty lots where the rubble of the neighboring hovels completely demolished by time had accumulated.

"Here it is," said Rezk, pointing to the door.

Samaraï seemed flabbergasted by this rapid arrival at their destination. He glanced at the door, then raised his eyes to the rooftop as if he were looking for a construction defect, a crack in the façade, the smallest risk of collapse of a kind that would prevent him from going in. True, there was nothing seductive about the house, but it was quite obviously solid on its foundation. Samaraï turned to Rezk and said, with a strain of terror in his voice:

"Don't you want to accompany me? You'll be my guest, you are a brother. Come, we'll talk about women and about love. It's a very mysterious subject, don't you think? I'd like to discuss it with you."

"I thank you, but it's quite impossible," said Rezk apologetically. "They're waiting for me at home. Really, I am terribly sorry to leave you."

Suddenly filled with remorse, Rezk was hesitant to go. He had a premonition that danger awaited the veterinary student behind the blood-colored door; it weighed on his conscience and made leaving seem like an act of treachery. They remained motionless for a long time, staring at each other, like two travelers meeting in a strange place, fascinated by the fluke of the encounter. Then abruptly

Samaraï stood up straight, seemed to regain his pride and his energy, and said in a voice that was firm but fraught with terrible melancholy:

"So, then, farewell, my brother!"

He dashed toward the brothel door with the rage of a man fleeing a vengeful fate, opened it, then slammed it noisily behind him.

The noise echoed through the neighborhood like a voice of misery wailing in a world of iniquity, and Rezk had the foreboding that his companion of a moment before had just vanished forever. He was still thinking about the enormous sum of money Samaraï kept in his pocket that made him so vulnerable. Then, all of a sudden, he grasped the danger of his own situation. He was now completely alone as he wended his way along these narrow, twisting alleys that were more macabre than a cemetery of infidels, and it seemed to him that the dubious shadows cast against the high walls moved with him as he passed by. Although his poverty—visible even to a blind man—had the ability to move the most ferocious murderer to pity, for the first time that night he felt fear clutch at him like a bony old woman and he began to run toward the square whose faint lights in the distance seemed to promise mad merrymaking. The tall streetlamps on their steel stems poured their moribund light down on the immutable peasant woman standing on her pedestal, her hand still stretching toward the horizon, her face fixed in stone reflecting the boundless futility of her gesture. Rezk stopped, relieved to have arrived without incident in this tolerably civilized part of town. It was not yet his time to die; he still needed to live in order to see just how far man's infamy could brazenly spread beneath the sun without provoking the slightest outcry from the universe. His hatred of Chawki was the scourge and bane of his existence, but it was also his talisman against forgetting all the disparaged miseries and humiliations. As if the intensity of his hatred had caused the living image of this despised individual to materialize in front of him, Rezk thought he recognized Chawki crossing the square at a quick tempo, a black satin cape draped around his shoulders, like a disoriented vampire. He was swinging his cane as if it were a weapon and moving from one streetlamp to another as though trying to follow a projector's brightly lit path. Rezk froze with surprise and for a moment thought he was seeing a mirage, a kind of provocation of his suffering; then he leapt with catlike agility on to the dusty ground of the vast square. He drew closer and closer to the man in the cape but, unlike that man, who sought out the light of the streetlamps, Rezk slipped cautiously into the patches of shadow, careful not to show himself. Even from behind and despite the ridiculous way he hopped about—a complete breach with the formal, stilted gait he used in public—Chawki stood out among all the other criminals of his class by a vileness so complete that it saturated the air around him. Rezk's instinct had not been wrong; it was indeed Chawki heading toward some dark destination. Rezk had simply allowed himself to get swept away; in his zeal he had not yet thought through what he was going to do. He was frightened by whatever it was that had driven him to this pursuit, and by some unformulated notion that was developing on its own, outside

172

of him, vesting him with a purificatory power. Was he going to appoint himself executioner and eliminate Chawki, kill him right then on this isolated square, with as sole witness that hideous statue, symbol of resurrection? But could destroying this prosperous bastard—a highly justified act—obliterate everything else? In any case, Rezk knew he was incapable of violence and rejected the idea with disgust. Most pathetically, he was starting to feel sorry for Chawki.

Chawki was skillfully navigating toward the sources of light while frantically waving his cane so as to scare off invisible demons. His goal now was not to parade himself in front of a backward people, but to reach, as quickly as possible, Imtaz's house, where special festivities were to take place in his honor. For the moment, his concern was to stay out of the shadows and not be mistaken for a common capitalist by brazen assailants. It was his massive smugness and his belief that the esteem in which the entire city held him made him untouchable that had dictated this particular course of action. Even the lowliest scoundrels would hesitate to disrespect such a highly placed person. But like all courses of action, this one was not devoid of a certain stupidity; it wasn't entirely impossible that the kidnappers or other evil-minded dregs of humanity were ignorant peasants straight out of their countryside and thus totally unaware of Chawki's position as an esthete and illustrious notable. If this were the case, it would obviously be sheer lunacy to show himself in the light. He was exasperated by this quandary that called upon his speculative faculties, and that tremendous anxiety was preventing him from resolving. The lewd, stirring image of the young schoolgirl from a good family waiting for him at Imtaz's house set his flesh ablaze almost to the point of orgasm and made even more dreadful the possibility of some mortal danger that would deprive him of a prey he had so fervently coveted just when he was about to do with it as he pleased. Spurred on by his depraved predilections, he hoped to find in this barely nubile child the innocent offspring of a family of his acquaintance, as if by sleeping with the daughter he would at the same time absorb the respectability of her parents, and he anticipated a positive influence on his waning virility from this act of sacrilege. As it happened, his sensuous nature had recently begun to show some signs of flagging that necessitated the use of various aphrodisiacs. There was a good chance that the young girl was still a virgin, and Chawki felt his stomach clench on realizing he had forgotten to supply himself with the life-saving drug. And so his most terrible fear was coming true: possessing the girl was becoming an intrepid task in all likelihood doomed to fail. But it was too late now to remedy his oversight. To go back the way he'd come, after suffering so many torments, demanded an amount of courage and daring he could no longer even imagine. Despite the fact that he was constantly quickening his pace, it seemed to him that he was barely moving forward, and that the former actor's house existed only in his mind, a mind overexcited by the vision of the young schoolgirl waiting for him naked on a bed in an obscene pose. This feeling was analogous to what he experienced in his nightmares when, hunted down by his former mistress, the irascible Salma—transformed for the occasion into a devouring female whose mouth dripped blood—he fled, but with the alarming sensation that however much he tried to accelerate the movements of his legs, rather than carrying him farther from the hideous creature, they were only decreasing the distance between them. Then his thoughts were flooded with malicious joy at the idea that from now on he was safe from the young woman and her abominable fulminations. What a blessing that this veterinary student had wound up there; that imbecile had done him a great favor by attacking him. What cheered Chawki most in this matter was that he would no longer have to pay an allowance or offer gifts to a woman who had ceased to play any part in his sexual fantasies. He was thinking about this with glee in the depths of his miserliness when suddenly his attention was drawn to a faint dancing light, very much like a ray of sunlight reflected in a mirror, and which he assumed was the reflection of a knife blade brandished above his neck by some individual standing behind him. For a brief instant he remained motionless, under a spell of terrible indecisiveness. Then, twirling his cane, he turned around to fight off the fatal stroke that was about to obliterate him. At that moment the phenomenon reoccurred with incredible speed—a tiny glimmer flittering in every direction—and he managed to locate its origin. He had been too quick to lose his head; the glimmer was coming from the ring he wore on his right hand, the one that held the cane; its stone glittered as soon as it caught a hint of light. Before Chawki had gone out, recalling

Imtaz's advice, he'd managed to take off all his rings except one that remained embedded in his flesh despite his struggles to remove it. It was a very valuable ring, with a large diamond that blazed like fire and that in all probability signaled his approach for miles around. He tried to hide his hand beneath the cloth of his cape, but this made it impossible for him to defend himself efficiently; his left hand was too clumsy to handle the cane in a fight for his life. This new worry threw him into indescribable confusion and only half-consciously did his eye perceive a human shape threading its way stealthily through the shadows. An icy shiver ran through Chawki as his gaze swept over the square intently seeking a section of wall or a tree trunk as shelter in his hasty retreat; all he found was the statue's plinth. He took a deep breath, then ran toward this monument to deceit; since it belonged to the government, in his mind it was obliged to protect him from envious men and outcasts. His body pressing against this feeble rampart like a fly on a sticky windowpane, his cane raised above his head in a final burst of heroism, he held his breath and listened carefully for the intruder's footsteps. After a moment, hearing nothing, he edged out from behind the pedestal and what he saw crushed his last hope of resistance. A man was heading calmly toward the statue with the satisfied air of an assassin confident in his strength and convinced that his victim had no chance of escape. Chawki would have liked to cry for help, to wake the entire city with a horrific roar, but either because the difficulties of this night had made him lose his voice or because his social standing forbade him from resorting to such unseemly extremes, no sound emerged from his throat. His fright, however, vanished all at once as soon as he could make out his pursuer's tiny figure. The anemic appearance and rough clothing of this odd stroller were evidence of undeniable poverty. Chawki felt reborn. The man could not be dangerous in the least; Chawki could easily get the better of him with a few well-dealt blows of his cane. With the courage of the coward faced with someone weaker than himself, he rushed out all aquiver from behind the pedestal, cane raised, ready to knock senseless this poor wretch who looked anything but ferocious.

Rezk had guessed what Chawki was up to and concluded that he had no more need to be discreet because in all likelihood his enemy was fully aware of his presence. So he'd walked on without trying to hide and, truth be told, rather unsure of the proper course of action to take in such circumstances. But seeing Chawki come out of his impromptu hiding place threatening him with his cane, he recoiled ever so slightly, disoriented by a move he had not expected.

Emboldened by this retreat, Chawki took advantage of his initial success and the superiority of his arsenal. He opened his arms wide as if to block Rezk's passage and cried in the incensed tones of a bank security guard shouting at a prowler:

"Who are you? And why are you following me?"

These questions increased Rezk's confusion and it took him a moment to respond, which he did contritely:

"I was not following you, Excellency."

The humility in this voice and the respect paid to his social status convinced Chawki of the young man's peaceful nature. Seeing him trembling with cold in his too-meager clothing, Chawki imagined that Rezk was frightened by the commanding authority that radiated from his person. Face to face with this worm, he was terribly annoyed at himself for his earlier fright. He lowered his cane and leaned on it, then, puffing out his chest, he began to fiddle with the ends of his moustache while scrutinizing Rezk's face with his usual arrogance. This face reminded him of some recent event.

"I seem to have seen you before. You were speaking to a young girl on a bicycle. It was yesterday afternoon, wasn't it?"

"It was," admitted Rezk in a conciliatory, almost obsequious tone that had the effect of making Chawki regain all his smugness.

"She is a lovely girl," he said. "You must have a fine time with her."

The image of the young girl of whom he had caught a quick glimpse astride her bicycle, her skirt sliding up her thighs, brought a perverse smile to Chawki's lips that Rezk understood as an insult to his sister's virtue. The young man was once again overcome by hatred and his eyes blazed. Chawki recognized this gaze that had shot through him the previous day and his suspicions returned.

"You don't remember me?" he asked sardonically. "I passed not far from you. I'm sure you noticed me."

"I don't recall. The street was very crowded."

"It doesn't matter. You were no doubt too taken with your pretty companion. Have you known her for a long time?"

"Yes, a very long time."

"How old was she when you met, then? She is still so young."

"I like them just barely out of childhood," said Rezk with a certain impertinence, as if he wanted to shock his interlocutor. "And you, Excellency?"

"Unquestionably, so do I," answered Chawki, casting a sidelong glance at the tireless statue frozen on her pedestal, witness to this impudent confession. "I see," he continued, "that despite appearances, you are a young man of quality. And to think that I mistook you for an ill-intentioned fellow. So, tell me about this girl on her bicycle."

Chawki was sliding into fetishism. The bicycle was exciting him more than anything else, he didn't know why.

"Ah, yes . . . the bicycle," sighed Rezk. "You have to see with what skill she steers that machine. She seems to fly though space, like an angel gliding above the squalid alleys—"

"How I would love to see this performance," interrupted Chawki, who was charmed by this poetic description as by a child's dream.

It seemed to Rezk that this polite conversation with his worst enemy was heading toward total absurdity. And although his hatred was becoming stronger, it was no longer based on vengeance—just on a kind of disgust, only a step away from the nothingness of death. But he would not kill the monster; he had found instead a means of torturing Chawki in his flesh by holding out the false promise of a meeting with Felfel. He could not repress a little inner laugh as he imagined Chawki's reaction to such a proposal.

"Would you like to see her in private?" he asked in a whisper.

Chawki reeled under the impact of this unexpected offer; he leaned more heavily on his cane and continued playing with his mustache, a look of dissolute sensuality spreading across his face.

"Really! You could manage to set up a meeting?"

Rezk fought the impulse to spit in his pompous face. He felt he was being put to a decisive test, and sensed that beneath the sham surface of this provincial potentate he had neglected an essential element: the innate ordinariness of the man. For an instant he was absorbed in contemplating the potbelly under the leafy-patterned vest; the sensualist's mouth twisted in a seductive pout; the big red rose in the buttonhole like a spreading splotch of fresh blood; the black satin cape—the classic, indispensable vampire accessory—cloaking the massive structure stuffed with fat. And suddenly, as if under the impact of some liberating trigger, Rezk's mind was overpowered by an obvious truth that left him dazed for a few seconds but filled him with breathtaking joy. He had just realized that Chawki, despite his ancestral wealth and the intangible power of his race, was nothing but a pitiable buffoon. How could he have despised this minstrel of a putrefying society and taken him so seriously? No doubt it was distance that lay at the root of this psychological error. Since his father's misadventure several years ago, Rezk had never come so close to Chawki, nor had he had occasion to study his degenerate features so thoroughly. From afar, Chawki had always seemed endowed with a demoniacal importance.

Rezk's laughter burst forth, splattering the night.

Chawki was waiting for his answer, frozen in his elegant pose, and this laughter came as a relief to him as well.

"She's my sister," said Rezk, who had stopped laughing.

It took Chawki a moment to grasp the significance of this confession.

"What?" he stammered, slightly aghast. (Then, in a bantering tone:) "Well, that's fantastic; it makes everything easier. Obviously you will be rewarded for your trouble. I'm very respected in this city; you can count on my complete discretion."

"I am at your service," answered Rezk maliciously. "Whenever you'd like, Excellency."

Rezk's sarcasm and flippancy remained imperceptible to Chawki, who was totally captivated by the way this extraordinary adventure had played out.

"I see that we understand one another. I am very pleased to have made the acquaintance of such a reasonable boy; it's so rare these days. Come see me; here's my address."

He pulled his card from a vest pocket and held it out to Rezk as if he were giving a coin to a beggar. With the respect due a precious object for which he would feel almost unworthy, Rezk took it. Regaining all his self-confidence, Chawki strode boldly away and, making his way to Imtaz's house, he rejoiced at how easily he had just added to his conquests.

The young whore was totally unrecognizable. Dressed in the smock purchased the previous day at a dry-goods store, her face thoroughly cleansed and a yellow ribbon around her hair falling in a thick braid down her back, she looked more like a schoolgirl than a schoolgirl. Her own mother wouldn't have recognized her, nor, especially, could Chawki, who had never ventured into the brothel where she was the magnificent resident. Lingering over some final touches and drinking champagne from tea-cups, the three young men who were the architects of her metamorphosis guffawed at the phenomenal success of their prank. The girl, amused at first, now seemed sorrowfully resigned, as if she missed her pretty sequined dress and tawdry jewelry that Imtaz had locked away in the wardrobe, or as if she had found deep within her some disturbing memory of her childhood. Impenetrable to this kind of humor, her mind could not understand all the childish exuberance the young men displayed. She was totally illiterate and this ritual in which she was being forced to take part aroused in her nothing but a listless torpor. Seated at the table in the middle of the bedroom, she was letting herself be guided in her role as a studious pupil, gazing helplessly at the schoolbook open before her, the notebook placed to the right, the pen held between her ink-stained fingers. She was angry with Medhat for having inflicted these humiliating marks on her, which would require intense scrubbing to remove. But Medhat, finicky artist that he was, had been determined to make his work look authentic, claiming that these ink-stained hands, in addition to being proof positive of her schoolgirl status, had the extra attribute of being a stimulant to the senses. This explanation did not make the girl any less morose.

When the front bell rang, Imtaz went to the door and ushered Chawki into the living room.

"Is she here?" inquired Chawki softly.

"Look," whispered Imtaz, pointing to the door that opened on the bedroom. "She's doing her homework."

Indeed, by some cleverly calculated staging, the girl could be seen from the living room sitting at the table, the lamp shining down on her head as she leaned pensively over her schoolbook.

"God help me!" sighed Chawki, sent into raptures by this tableau.

"As you can see, she's a serious girl who doesn't waste her time," added Medhat.

"She's first in her class," said Teymour, going Medhat one better.

"I don't know how to thank you," said Chawki, curbing the arrogant inflection of his voice. "It's all too splendid!"

"Nothing's too good for a friend like you," said Imtaz, bowing. "And now, go on; she's waiting for you."

Just then the girl turned her head in their direction and smiled impishly and tenderly, which had a tremendous effect on Chawki. As he entered the bedroom he felt as if a mysterious magician were ushering him in to an eternity of debauchery.

: VIII :

IT WAS ONLY TEN O'CLOCK in the morning and, apart
from a handful of open shops and a few street peddlers
hawking their wares in voices that were still shaky, the city
remained sunk in drowsiness. In its futile attempt to dry
the streets that were damp from the previous day's rain,
a hazy sun was making the water that had collected in the
potholes glisten. Medhat walked falteringly, his mind still
dull with sleep; he was fundamentally allergic to this entire early morning atmosphere. As he headed for Salma's,
he wondered what emergency required him to call on her at
such an ungodly hour. The little servant girl who had come
to pull him out of bed had urged him to go see her mistress
straight away; Salma had even ordered her to "take him by
the hand" should he put up any resistance. Medhat smiled
at this expression of pure formality, knowing that the little servant, a girl of about twelve, had a distinct fondness
for him, as if he were some fashionable new sweetmeat.
She had wanted to carry out her mission to the letter and
had tried to grab his hand, but he'd called her, jestingly, a
vile seductress and urged her to be off without waiting for

him. The girl looked at him disdainfully, then went on her way, slightly saddened by her defeat. Medhat knew it was all an act, and that at the next opportunity she would be even more flirtatious. At heart, she amused him quite a bit and he thought that in a year or two she would be ripe for a more serious game. He had a gift for spotting girls who had not yet reached puberty but who showed all the signs of precocious sensuality; he maintained adult relationships with them, keeping them in a state of emotional receptivity during the entire process of their transformation by serving them up an assortment of adoring glances, flattering remarks, and phony fits of jealousy until they reached a suitable age. Since female youth was a very perishable good, it seemed of real importance to lay the groundwork for the future.

Salma's request was particularly worrisome because in all probability it had to do with some new dispute between her and that cursèd Samaraï; his crude and unrestrained passion was making him unbearable. Had he attempted to strangle her? Anything was possible from such an unenlightened person; he was practically a savage. Medhat had lost all interest in the veterinary student as soon as he realized how wrong he had been about him. His unfailing ability to size up people had been proved seriously flawed by this monster of ingratitude, this bleating lover who, not content simply to betray Medhat's trust, was also behaving like a boor in a friend's home. When Medhat met Samaraï for the first time, he thought he would be doing a good deed by leading this hopelessly stupid lackey of the bourgeoisie away from a mediocre and insipid fate. But it had turned out that Samaraï was fiercely determined to continue his studies and get his degree, demonstrating thereby his total lunacy. He was the sort of boy who was beyond redemption, wholly in thrall to the idiocy of the times, and Medhat had, as casually as always, struck him from his list of acquaintances.

Unfortunately, Medhat had committed an even more serious blunder and harmed another person by introducing Samaraï to Salma. The hardship she suffered from the intrusion of this individual in her life—with his retrograde ideas of love as tragedy—was of personal concern to Medhat, given that he was solely responsible for it. He should have known better; a man infatuated with diplomas was someone to be avoided like the plague. Medhat could not forgive himself for this mistake, for it affected an understanding and generous woman who alone was worth all the students in all the universities in the world.

This led him to think about Teymour and how he had judged him when he first returned from abroad. Contrary to Medhat's hasty judgment, however, Teymour had revealed himself to be wonderfully clever; he had done nothing but amuse himself over there and his diploma was not a degrading document, but a forgery obtained in exchange for money in order to reassure his family. His admiration for Teymour increased at this thought and he recalled that, having found a place to live in the old city, Teymour was planning on holding a party soon. Medhat suddenly forgot the quarrels between Salma and her tortuous lover and began to consider whom among his female acquaintances he would choose to liven up the festivities.

Salma was waiting for him in the kitchen, seated with a cup of coffee in front of her.

"It took you a long time to get here, son of a dog!" she shouted as soon as she saw him. "I cannot count on anyone in this city. Especially not on you, the cause of all my woes!"

Medhat sat facing her, imperturbably calm; he was now certain that at the root of this summons lay some misdeed on the part of the veterinary student. He stretched out his legs, leaned back in his chair, relaxed, and waited patiently to hear the young woman's grievances. The little servant girl, washing dishes at the sink, was pretending to ignore him. Medhat, too, had turned his gaze from her and seemed entirely uninterested in her presence in the kitchen. It was the slowest and most arousing game, this game of pretending to ignore each other.

"What's wrong?" he asked, as if he knew nothing.

The hypocrisy of this question enraged Salma, who withdrew into hostile silence. She wanted to punish the young man for his impertinence by plunging him in the throes of uncertainty. But Medhat always encouraged this very feminine fondness for ambiguous situations because it gave him time to daydream about frivolous things while simulating the signs of restless expectation. In fact he could only consider Salma's inconsolable distress with detachment, as an infinitesimal part of the general chaos with which he refused to compromise. With her disheveled hair, her make-up watered by tears, and the distraught fixedness of her reddened eyes, she looked like a witch in a trance. After a minute she seemed to recall that there was no point in laying claim to martyrdom with Medhat; tragedy amused him the same way a puppet show did.

Emerging from her silence, she cried:

"Where is he, that pimp?"

"Samaraï? What did he do now?"

"He disappeared four days ago, that's what he did. What does he think, that louse? My house is not a hotel!"

"So he's gone!" Medhat cried. "What good news!"

"He's not gone; his suitcase is still here. He's probably hanging around the city somewhere. He must have found another fool like me to put him up. You! You must know where he is."

"On my honor, I know nothing," Medhat said. "I haven't seen him since the evening he quarreled with Chawki."

"Is that true? Swear it!"

"I swear. And I can also tell you that I'm happy to be rid of him. He's the type of person who needs to live in the capital. An ambitious man can only move in a world of other ambitious men. The capital is swarming with civil servants awaiting promotion. Believe me. He's gone back to his quagmire."

"I'm telling you, he hasn't gone; he would never have left his suitcase behind. He's not like you; his things matter a great deal to him. He takes pride in ownership. I've seen him sick with grief because he lost one of his handker-chiefs. Apparently it was a gift from his mother."

Tears were now streaming down her cheeks. She seemed sorely afflicted by her lover's running away.

"Hankering for a handkerchief," said Medhat with

commiseration. "That doesn't surprise me. What you just told me merely confirms my opinion."

Salma said no more, but this time her silence was not heavy with the rancor and bitterness that had put Medhat on the defensive. She looked at him doubtfully, as if she were attempting to understand things with which she had had no contact for many long years. A loving, tragic anxiety could be read in her eyes. She'd wound up growing fond of Samaraï and his ardent, fanatical love that had remained a mystery to her, and to which she was hardly accustomed. Over the past few days she had felt alone, abandoned by everyone. She became aware of an emptiness caused by Samaraï's absence, a void that even her hatred of Chawki could not fill; she now regretted not having listened to her unhappy lover's proposals and having been cantankerous and vindictive with the only person who had thought about saving her from her self-destructive folly. Perhaps she should have left this city, forgotten her lost youth and the man who had taken advantage of her, to begin a new life elsewhere. She was already twenty-two, and the veterinary student had been her last chance to renounce her status as a dishonored girl and abandon her extravagant quest for an illusory revenge. But now it was too late. She was overcome with dread at the thought of the person who had vanished; she could not dissociate his disappearance from the recent kidnappings in the city. Already she could picture her lover dead, his corpse dismembered and rendered unrecognizable, lying among the rubble of some wasteland. Once again this vision made her shiver; she readjusted the collar of her dressing gown around her breasts, then asked in a low and trembling voice, as if she feared divulging her secret foreboding:

"Do you think he may have had an accident? Could he have been kidnapped like all those other notables of whom we've never found a trace?"

Medhat began to laugh. It seemed to him that Salma was going much too far, exaggerating the tragedy out of sheer feminine vanity.

"But that poor fellow is no notable. No one would think of kidnapping him. He would very quickly become a burden to his kidnappers. I would not want to be in their shoes."

"You're forgetting that he always carried on his person all that money he'd inherited."

The sudden surfacing of this detail made Medhat oddly attentive. Samaraï's disappearance was taking on new meaning. It was true; Samaraï carried his entire fortune everywhere he went. Medhat had noticed it several times, but had forgotten. In this light, the kidnapping seemed entirely plausible. He could not help but see something epically comic in the idea that the veterinary student had ended his career in this way. He snickered, finding the situation quite humorous.

"Well, that's one less veterinarian in this country. But what does it matter? I'm sure the animals won't suffer from such a loss."

"Still, he was your friend!" cried Salma. "You were the one who brought him here and introduced him to me as a delightful companion and a brother. You seemed so concerned about making life pleasant for him. On top of it, you tried desperately to convince him not to go back to the capital, as if you were in love with him! I don't understand your reaction now that he may be dead."

She began to cry softly, which irritated Medhat; really, this was not a spectacle to inflict on him so early in the morning. He had admitted his disappointment in Samaraï to Salma, and now seemed the appropriate time to reveal the heinous truth about her lover's outmoded and stupid mentality. Medhat was not going to let himself be persecuted in this way without reacting.

"I never told you, but I made a mistake. I thought he would be a positive element in our group. I took him for an intelligent boy, able to grasp all the childishness of his smug pursuit of a degree in veterinary medicine. At first he gave me the impression he had understood, but that was just show. In truth he simply wanted a few days of vacation and had nothing against sleeping with you as a bonus. He had never seen a thing in his life, that peasant! Rather than behaving properly and savoring such simple happiness, he had the cheek to want to take you away with him to live in the capital. The height of ingratitude! In short, he disappointed me and I refuse to fret over this imbecile any longer. In any case, nothing has happened to him; that would be too much to hope for."

"It's all my fault. I chased him away. What will become of me if they've killed him? Tell me, how could I go on living?"

It was difficult to quell Medhat's optimism with words of this sort. He, too, knew how to exploit the rules of tragedy and he made sure to give a comforting and even slightly mundane tone to his own lines of dialogue:

"Don't worry. He's probably getting drunk somewhere. I'm sure he'll be back soon."

"Try to find him. Tell him I forgive him everything and he can come back."

In spite of himself, Medhat was touched by this unforeseeable change of mind. Until now he had always thought that Salma tolerated the veterinary student like some inevitable curse and that she had nothing but scorn for his turbulent passion. But Samaraï's disappearance was turning her into a tearful lover admitting her faults and ready to forgive all transgressions. Had she by chance begun to love Samaraï, or on this occasion was she resorting to just another subterfuge because of her constant need to play an ill-starred role in her relations with men? How could one know? It was as pointless to try to penetrate the unbalanced mind of a woman as it was to attempt to read the future in coffee grounds. In any case, Medhat had had enough of this funeral. All he wanted was never to see the veterinary student again. Still, he said:

"You can count on me. I'll start looking for him right away."

He made as if to get up from his chair, but Salma reached out her arm to hold him back.

"Stay and have lunch with me. I don't feel like being alone."

He was about to decline the invitation when the little servant girl who was feverishly drying the dishes at the sink shot a quick glance his way, as if she were expecting him to accept. Medhat caught this glance and said joyfully:

"Of course, with pleasure."

The young servant girl's body trembled ever so slightly and Medhat looked forward with glee to all the teasing that would go on between them during lunch. Lost in the pain of her putative widowhood, Salma suspected nothing.

The morning sun had vanished by the time Medhat left Salma's house. A gray sky darkened the alleys emptied at siesta time, and he wondered how he should spend his afternoon. He had promised the young woman to look for Samaraï in every nook and cranny of the city, but in truth, for him everything was simple, everything had been resolved long ago. The affairs of this world had no influence—good or bad—on Medhat's behavior. The veterinary student was merely a fleeting episode, a tiny insignificant blemish, not vital in the least. It was one of life's imponderables, like when one slips and breaks a leg or when one realizes in the middle of screwing a girl that she's older than one thought. Still, he could not manage to shake the event from his mind completely. Samaraï, by running away like this—without saying goodbye or thank you—would forever remain a mystery, disturbing the peaceful course of all their lives and fueling his legend by his heroic death. It might in fact be necessary to find Samaraï's hiding place, if only to put an end to the malicious rumors and to discredit the cheap romanticism that his absence was creating in Salma's mind. The probability of a kidnapping by unknown hooligans who were stripping the city of its notables seemed rather slim to Medhat, despite the lure of the inheritance money that this improvident capitalist carried around in his pocket as if it were a packet of peanuts. Medhat decided that he needed to discuss the problem with Teymour and headed toward the new lodgings rented a short while ago across the river. The place was in his own neighborhood, but he had yet to visit it.

Crossing the river on the iron bridge, Medhat caught sight of young Rezk leaning on the parapet, discreetly nibbling something held tightly in his hand. He seemed deep in contemplation of the landscape. Enchanted by this coincidence, Medhat approached the young man, muffling the sound of his footsteps—he wanted to surprise him—then came to a halt next to him. Rezk was finishing up a honey cake; he wiped his fingers with the paper in which the pastry had been wrapped, made it into a ball, and tossed it in the river. Then he turned around and saw Medhat gazing at him with his odd benevolence and a touch of irony.

"What a fortunate encounter!" he said looking Medhat straight in the eye, contrary to his habit. "As God is my witness, I wanted nothing more."

He seemed exhilarated to be alive, and it was the first time Medhat had ever seen this smiling face on him. He had lost his sickly air, and his still youthful features were bathed with insolent joy.

Medhat was momentarily stunned by the police informant's new personality; Rezk had hardly accustomed him to such warm relations. Over the course of their various encounters, he had felt a reticence in Rezk, a kind of guilty shyness, and he had always tried to break through the barriers that the young man—for an obvious reason, but one which Medhat found trivial—contrived to erect between them. So what had happened to him? Medhat was honestly intrigued. The veterinary student's escapade and Salma's hysterical sniveling seemed trifling compared to the mystery of the surprising transformation of the young police informant. And so the absurd idea of going to look for Samaraï, lost in some disreputable joint, immediately went out of his head. He placed his hand on Rezk's shoulder, trying to communicate through this touch that he was very sensitive to his signs of friendship.

"I'm so happy to see you Rezk, my brother! Out for a stroll, are you?"

"This is the best time of day. All the shops are closed and the people are taking their siestas. I like to be out walking when no one else is about. I particularly like to linger on this bridge and contemplate the swirling river. There is a lot of poetry in this river, don't you think? In fact, this city is filled with delightful landscapes. Even its houses, tumbledown and crumbling on the surface, possess a certain charm. But who notices?"

He spoke almost lyrically and his features expressed an entirely new elation. Medhat was dazzled by the flame shooting out of his ordinarily lackluster eyes. His sudden violent love for the eternal splendors of nature astounded Medhat, as if the young man had fathomed a secret of which he, Medhat, had been the sole guardian.

"I do," he said. "I've always noticed. You're right. There

are unsuspected beauties in this city."

Rezk seemed to hesitate; then he said, with the embarrassment of a young girl confessing her passion to a stranger:

"Do you know that I was thinking of you a while ago?"

"You fill me with honor! May I ask why?"

"Precisely in regard to this city. I know you like it here. You are the only person among my acquaintances who seems to love this city with all his heart. It's as if you had found an inexhaustible source of joy here. I confess that for a long time this seemed incomprehensible to me. I realize now that I was simply blind."

"My dear Rezk, not every man is capable of appreciating what is around him. Most men imagine they will find what they are seeking somewhere else, and yet it is right in front of them, laid out under their very eyes."

"I, too, was like that. But I had an excuse, and I can tell *you* what it was. It was my hatred of one man that blinded me. This hatred weighed on me like a curse. It took me years to put it out my mind."

"What do you mean?"

Rezk giggled, as if Medhat must already have known the answer and had merely asked the question to be polite.

"I realized that this man was no more than a buffoon."

"It took you so many years to figure that out! But all men are buffoons. Bloodthirsty buffoons, but buffoons nonetheless. Well, congratulations."

So that was the explanation. Medhat did not ask who it was who had deserved such dogged hate. It could be anyone. The majority of humanity was quite obviously hateful to anyone who had once indulged in a belief in mankind. And poor Rezk had believed, inevitably.

"I was sure you would understand."

"Why were you so sure? You don't really know anything about me. We've never had the chance to talk."

"You don't know it, but I am aware of many things that have to do with you. In truth, I have great admiration for you and your friends. I consider you to be the only living beings in this city."

"Why, then, did you always avoid me? Was I ever disdainful or indifferent to you?"

"Quite the opposite. You have always been remarkably noble. I admit the fault is mine. But I wasn't avoiding you. It's just that circumstances were not favorable. . . . And it was a matter of conscience . . . I was reluctant to commit an act of disloyalty . . ."

Now that the mystery of Rezk's bizarre behavior had been cleared up, Medhat would have liked to urge his companion to be more open, and to take advantage of his confessional mood to force out of him some hint as to the mental state of the police who suspected him and his friends of being dangerous revolutionaries. Rezk was the one who'd been appointed to keep an eye on them and he was aware of almost everything they'd done. Why, then, did Hillali, knowing their innocence, persist in believing they were plotting against the government? This was one of the police chief's many eccentricities that Medhat had long wanted to comprehend. But he had to act prudently and above all not scare off the young man with questions that were too forthright.

"I don't see where the disloyalty is," he said with mischievous simplicity.

"One day I'll tell you everything, and I hope you will forgive me."

Rezk's tone had become serious, and the joyful flame in his eyes had gone out. Medhat took pity on him; he smiled and once again patted him on the shoulder.

"I know everything, Rezk, my brother! And I have nothing to forgive you for."

Rezk's countenance showed neither surprise nor the mortifying pallor of someone accused of treason, but rather an air of sweet deliverance, as if at last the mask had fallen and he could now show his true face. With a kind of calm resignation, he said:

"So, you knew. I should have realized it."

"Yes, I knew you were working for the police. But it doesn't matter! I also know what a man is reduced to in order to earn his daily bread. Your profession is no different from any other. By whatever means you participate in this despicable world, even by the tiniest job, you inevitably betray someone. We live in a society based on betrayal. That's why your job as an informant never seemed dishonorable to me. I've always liked you."

"I don't understand. You knew what I did and yet you did not despise me!"

"One's got to survive. In any case, you couldn't harm us. You have too much integrity to tell the police chief nonsense, like an ordinary informant filling his report with unverifiable rubbish in order to make himself look good. You could only tell the truth. With you, we were sure to be able to prove our good behavior. You were in a position to know we weren't plotting against the government in any way."

"That's what I always told the police chief. But he never wanted to believe me. He claimed I was too naïve when I'd say that all you were thinking about was sleeping with girls and having a good time."

"And this didn't seem odd to you?"

Rezk turned around slowly and leaned his elbows on the parapet, then began to look at the river in silence. He had thought a lot about the question preoccupying Medhat and he had reached the conclusion that the police chief, for personal reasons, had decided that this city was concealing a revolutionary organization. Hillali's insistence on supporting his hypothesis about a plot hatched by these young men to overthrow the government could only stem from some mental decline caused by his thwarted ambition. This cruel and cynical analysis of a man whom he revered shocked Rezk's sense of honor, but he found himself forced into this ultimate betrayal. He felt obligated to give Medhat an explanation that would clarify his true role in the whole affair and exonerate him from eternal shame. He was convinced that this explanation would meet with Medhat's approval, since Medhat was by nature prone to admiring the absurd side of all human undertakings.

"I think you are his drug."

"What do you mean?"

"I'm sure you know that he was assigned to this city only a few years ago. Before, he held an important position in the capital. So the old man is bored. He can't get used to it here."

"Don't tell me he's inventing conspiracies to amuse himself!"

"No, not exactly. He thinks his job as chief of police in a small city like ours is a disgrace and a travesty. He is a man of superior intelligence who constantly needs to put his intellectual faculties to the test. Ordinary thieves and murderers don't interest him; in his job, that sort of delinquent can only offer him the sad privilege of investigating the basest instincts of the rabble. He would like to be able to fight more refined criminals, ones motivated not by lucre but by some political ideal: an invisible and crafty enemy advocating disorder and violence worthy of his deliberation. I don't think his goal is a selfish one, or that he wants to take credit for some spectacular action by quashing a conspiracy in the hopes of earning the government's gratitude. I know him well enough to be sure that he is very contemptuous of the men in power. His only aim is to dwell in a place inhabited by living souls. In his mind, a city without revolutionaries is a dead city, or simply a city without history."

"Does he realize how absurd that is?"

"No, not at all. He truly believes there is a conspiracy. It's even his main preoccupation."

"How extraordinary! I am enchanted by what you've just told me. I suspected something, but I never imagined that. Tell me, does he also think we are responsible for the notables' disappearance?"

"Of course. These disappearances have convinced him that the movement has grown and is beginning to act. He's reading loads of books about revolutionary strategies."

"Well, good for him. He should continue to do so; I don't see any problem in that. To each his own amusement. Tolerance is my first rule of conduct."

Although he was well aware of the prevailing stupidity, Medhat, despite his feigned indifference, was somewhat surprised by all this. The unbelievably ridiculous ideas of this man in a position of great responsibility proved, if proof were still necessary, the frailty of a system collapsing beneath the weight of its iniquities. This Hillali, who had accepted the sham, worked for it, and built his career on deceitful foundations and ethics, was now trapped in his old age, inventing another form of sham to extend his flagging authority. For him and his ilk—thoroughgoing cheats all—the moment of retirement also meant the terrible failure of their dreams. This is how dogs that have been abandoned by their masters die, having hunted in vain for a bone to gnaw on in the trashcans of strangers. Medhat, too, leaned on the parapet and looked at the river. In the distance, a sailboat was fighting against the current, its quivering sail leaning dangerously toward the hazy line of the horizon. Above some carrion on one of the banks, kite birds were circling—immutable raptors of the sky, more serene and more majestic than their competitors, men of the earth. The inordinate grayness of this landscape was so oppressive that Medhat sympathized with Hillali's distress; Hillali—who had been thrown back by his own kind into this decadent city and excluded from the splendors that would have been lavished upon him had he collaborated with the authorities—had nothing but the mirage of a conspiracy to fill his loneliness.

Through some subtle line of thought, Hillali's paranoid delusions led Medhat to recall Samaraï's disappearance, which he had completely forgotten. The idea that he had to fulfill his promise to Salma displeased him, and he thought it would be clever to take advantage of his new friendship with Rezk to find out more about this business, sparing him pointless effort. For his job, Rezk moved about a lot, and if the veterinary student were still in the city, perhaps he would have seen him during one of his harmless attempts at spying for the chief of police.

"By the way," said Medhat, "one of my friends has disappeared. I wonder if by any chance you haven't seen him."

"Which one?"

"The veterinary student. The one who came from the capital to claim his inheritance. You must have seen him, he accompanied me everywhere. His name is Samaraï."

"Yes, I know him. When did he disappear?"

"About four days ago. The person with whom he's been living is worried about him. I'd like to be able to reassure her."

"If I'm not mistaken, he was just passing through here. Perhaps he went back home? It seems logical to me."

"Unfortunately not. He didn't take any of his clothes. His suitcase is still here, and so are his medical books, which were very important to him and which he would never have abandoned if he had left for good."

"That's really strange."

"I think so, too. So, try to remember. Did you see him recently?"

Rezk's nighttime meeting with the veterinary student was too recent for him to pretend to be searching his memory. For anyone else, it would have been a chance, ordinary encounter and he should have mentioned it to Medhat without thinking; yet he remained paralyzed, as if gripped by some superstitious fear. It had been exactly four days since that unbelievable scene of their separation in front of the brothel door. The last image Rezk had of Samaraï rushing headlong like a doomed man at the blood-red door was still present in his mind. And the distress he had felt at the time gripped him once again, as if his premonition of a calamity had come true. But what calamity could befall a man in this brothel, a place meant for pleasure? Perhaps he was still there, lost in debauchery and oblivious to the outside world. Hadn't he proclaimed his intention of paying every woman in the place? Such ambitious sexual plans could occupy someone for several days, perhaps an entire month. There was nothing frightening about that; it seemed more likely that he had simply gone into hiding for a time.

"I saw him in fact just four days ago."

"Where?"

"On the street. At night. He stopped me to ask for directions. He was very drunk and his words defied common sense. I had the feeling he was terribly lovesick and was trying to forget his pain by doing something reckless."

"Where'd he want to go?"

"He was looking for Wataniya's brothel."

"Do you think he went there?"

"It was hard for me to explain how to go, especially since he was incapable of getting there by himself, so I accompanied him to the door. He invited me to come in with him, but I refused. He had a lot of money on him, and he showed it to me ostentatiously. It must have been his entire inheritance."

"And you haven't seen him again since that night?"

"No. He opened the door and slammed it behind him. I stayed outside, alone. I was worried because of all that money."

Medhat knit his brow and an odd glimmer came into his gaze, but he quickly turned his head so that Rezk could not discern the slightest trace of the suspicion that had just formed in his mind. Rezk's account threw a dazzling light on the mystery of those disappearances that were all over the city's news. It was in Wataniya's brothel—he was now convinced of it—that the notables were disappearing, and an ignorant police force, led by a megalomaniac chief, persisted in believing them to be the victims of a revolutionary conspiracy. He recalled that the owner was not alone in managing her profitable business; she had a husband to help her with her task, a phenomenally strong ex-convict with a physical appearance as noxious as his wife's, who lived in one of the bedrooms in the rear and who never showed himself in public. Between the two of them, it would be relatively easy to kill a rich client, and divest him of his money and his jewels. The house was surrounded by empty lots perfectly suitable for burying illicit corpses once they had been cut into pieces to prevent identification. The whole thing must have functioned like a factory, or a closed circuit, with no need of recourse to the outside world since the victims came of their own free will. Medhat almost burst out laughing, but he contained himself; he was not crazy enough to shout his discovery from the rooftops. Rezk especially must know nothing about it.

A line of camels, apparently without a driver, crossed the bridge, followed closely by a donkey cart carrying an assembly of female mourners on their way to a funeral, their grieving faces painted blue; from time to time, one of them would begin a series of short wails, like a singer warming up her voice before coming on stage. From farther away, about to drive on to the bridge, a rich man's calèche, clean and shiny, was approaching; its horse, a noble beast, was walking solemnly in quick time. Visibly, the city was waking up after its siesta. Medhat thought it was time for him to go.

"Well, Rezk, my brother, I'll say goodbye now! You have opened new horizons for me. I will not be quick to forget this interesting conversation."

"When will we see each other again?"

"Whenever you'd like. I'm always happy to see you; you know that."

"Listen, I want you to know something: I'm going to resign. Nothing will keep us from seeing each other after that. There won't be any mistrust between us anymore."

"There was never any mistrust on my part. In any case, that's good news, and I'm happy to hear it."

Before he left Rezk, Medhat held him tightly against his chest in a pledge of brotherly friendship. It was to Rezk that he owed his sensational discovery and he wanted to thank him in an even more demonstrative way. As he walked away, he turned around several times to smile at him.

Stretched out on a burlap-covered mattress on the floor, Teymour was dreaming of his young saltimbanque. There was nothing luxurious about the apartment that Felfel had found for him in the old city. It consisted of one fairly large room with a window that looked out on an alleyway and a small alcove that served as a kitchen. Teymour had furnished it with a hermit's attention to detail, taking only a few necessities from his father's house. Ever since he could come here on occasion to escape the family atmosphere, Teymour had been savoring a freedom that reminded him of his years abroad when he was pretending to study arduously and endlessly. Not that his father made him submit to any strict rules of behavior, or that he had to go along with any rites and customs which no longer meant anything to him, but he felt that he would be betraying young Felfel's guileless love were he to live in a physical comfort and bourgeois prosperity that distanced him spiritually from her. Old Teymour hardly criticized him for his life of leisure and had never again mentioned the chemical engineering position he had set aside for him in the sugar refinery; suffering from early senility, he seemed to have forgotten that his son, after a long stay in a distant country, had obtained a degree that placed him among the elite of his generation. The diploma was now hanging in a gilded wood frame on the wall just above Teymour's mattress, as if it were the very proof of the triumph of fraud. It was on seeing the naked walls of his pitiful lodgings that Teymour had had the clever idea of placing the phony diploma—fruit of a victory over himself and the dark forces of reaction—in full view of his visitors. Thus, at any moment he could contemplate this first-rate relic from his past that symbolized for him all the failings of the notorious values that govern this world. But most unexpected was the fact that exhibiting this diploma had helped spread his reputation even to the lowliest hovels. In effect, through his housekeeper— whose husband was a knife grinder—the entire neighborhood had become aware that he was a learned engineer, and this had earned him respectful nods and words of praise from all the wise and erudite men with which the city teemed as he passed in front of their doors or sat down in a café. Teymour was thrilled by his prestige among the people inasmuch as it offset the exorbitant price he had paid for the document. He congratulated himself for at last having derived some benefit from it.

He cast a sardonic glance at the frame hanging above him, then got up and went to look through the slats in the closed shutters at what was brewing on the streets. After a moment he was surprised to see Medhat appear, strolling casually with the alert and inquisitive concentration of someone roaming through an exotic market. He hurried to open the door to the landing, then came back to squat on the mattress, leaving the only chair for his guest.

It immediately struck Teymour that Medhat was very excited by some new fact and that he had come strictly with the intention of sharing it, but that he would not reveal it right away. In such circumstances Teymour knew it was pointless to rush Medhat; in the end he would talk without prompting. Medhat did not pretend to go into raptures about how beautiful the place was; still, he took the trouble to walk around the whole room—not in order to admire the nonexistent furniture, but out of courtesy to his host— and stopped in front of the diploma on the wall, studied it closely, then nodded his head in satisfaction.

"It's magnificent," he said. "Did it cost you a lot?"

"Yes, quite a lot. But you see it has its uses. It gives the room a studious air that keeps malicious gossip at bay. It is the guarantor of my respectability in the neighborhood."

"It was a good idea to hang it there. It's better than a work of art. Unfortunately, you can't sell it—your name is on it."

"I did think about it, though. But to whom would I sell it? We don't know any fool who wants a diploma."

"The only one we know has disappeared. And it wasn't a diploma in chemical engineering that he wanted, but one in veterinary medicine."

"Samaraï! How did he disappear?"

"In a completely honorable and definitive way: he died."

"When? I knew nothing about this. How did you find out?"

Medhat smiled at Teymour's incredulous air, but at the same time he seemed to regret having let himself walk into a trap in this way. He had inadvertently divulged his secret too quickly. Noticing the single chair, he sat down sighing, stretched his legs and began to stare at Teymour with gentle condescension. Then he recounted the whole story from beginning to end, from Salma's anguished appeal to him, to his meeting on the bridge with Rezk, and finally to his discovery, thanks to his own perspicacity, of the true assassins.

"What do you say to that? It was so simple, and yet nobody thought of it. Believe me, all those vanished notables went to Wataniya's. Most of them are rich hicks who come to the city to sell their crops or their cattle and who have a lot of cash on them, not to mention jewelry—gold rings and watch chains. Their first thought, once they've taken care of business, is to go have a good time in a brothel. And then it's child's play for Wataniya and her colossus of a husband to kill them and bury them in the empty lots that surround the house. I'm sure my reasoning is flawless."

"Fine," said Teymour, "but what are we going to do?"

"If you ask me, we're not going to do anything."

"You mean we're going to keep this to ourselves?"

"Naturally. It's none of our business. If bastards are killing other bastards, what does that have to do with us? You don't realize how lucky we are! We are going to sit back and quietly watch the slaughter of notables. Could there possibly be a more delightful spectacle?"

"In that case, I'm afraid it is our business. You'll see that it will not take long for Hillali to accuse us of Samaraï's disappearance. Samaraï was a friend of ours and he went around with us the whole time he was here. We will be questioned and possibly imprisoned."

"If he makes that mistake, he'll look ridiculous. We

didn't kill anyone. And first he'll need to find the corpse. Without a corpse he cannot begin the slightest proceedings against us. He is so obsessed with his political conspiracies that he'll never think of Wataniya's brothel. I wouldn't have thought of it myself if Rezk hadn't mentioned that he'd seen Samaraï go into the brothel with his entire inheritance in his pocket. That detail opened my eyes."

"Poor Samaraï. It's as if he were an innocent victim chosen by fate."

"I don't agree. Samaraï had a slave mentality. And slaves are not innocent. They collaborate in running this vast universal dupery. Deep down he only got what he deserved."

"He wasn't a bad guy."

"An ambitious guy is not a good guy for long. By getting his degree, Samaraï wanted to succeed in finding a place in this society we abhor. In a few years he would have become worse than everyone else. A self-important man about town."

"Perhaps," said Teymour, recalling Medhat's suspicion toward him, Teymour, when he had seen him come home with his diploma. "And that's what you thought of me when I returned from abroad."

"Not exactly. I trusted you. The friend I had known before could never stoop so low."

From the alleyway could be heard the harsh voice of a gossipmonger scolding her children with the hot-tempered extremism of poverty. Medhat listened to her enumerating the fatal illnesses that she wished on them and was dumbfounded by her knowledge in this field. There were some he had never even heard of, for they were new.

"She must listen to the radio," he thought. Then he turned back to Teymour and said:

"I never discussed it with you, but I want you to know that I was greatly relieved when I learned the truth about your exemplary conduct during those years of absence. You don't know how impatiently I waited for you to return. I cherished the hope that you would come back as pure and intransigent as you were before you left. I did not want to lose you."

"You doubted my strength of character. And yet you knew me better than anyone. How could I have fallen short of your expectations?"

"Stronger men than you have been appropriated by power. I was right to fear for you."

"I didn't go over there to learn anything. I already knew everything I wanted to know. But it was essential for me to realize that deceit is rife everywhere."

Medhat got out of his chair and took a few steps around the room. His agitation had subsided and he was reflecting calmly on their decision to keep their startling discovery to themselves. He had calculated all the risks, and even the possibility of their going to prison seemed a rather tempting experience.

"Even if we had to go to prison, I wouldn't mind. On the contrary, it would be a change from our routine. You can meet fantastic sorts in prison."

"I think we should tell Imtaz. I believe he'd share our view."

"We'll go to his house shortly. Then, tonight I intend to go to Wataniya's. I want to kiss her hand and thank her for everything she has done and will do in this city."

"Why would you want to kiss that horrible woman's hand?"

"Wouldn't you kiss the hand that rids you of the plague?"

"But this plague is endless. It would take more than those miserable assassinations. At this rate, it will take millions of years to get rid of it."

"Patience, my dear Teymour. I agree that it's a small-scale enterprise. But the bastards don't get along among themselves and they'll soon be killing each other from one end of the planet to another using vast and violent means. Still, we should not look down on those who are taking the initiative to begin the slaughter with their own meager means. The tiniest bomb that explodes somewhere should delight us, for behind the noise it makes when it explodes, even if barely audible, lies the laughter of a distant friend."

The afternoon was coming to an end and the gloomy winter dusk was stealing over the city as they set off for the former actor's house. Crossing the iron bridge, they were suddenly overcome with uncontrollable laughter and they began to run, turning in circles and chasing one another, filled with wonder at their freedom and as if intoxicated by the immensity of their fearsome secret. Soon, in the corner of the square, they came across a band of schoolboys kicking a ball around, and they heaped curses on them for participating in this stupid game that had been promoted as the ultimate social activity by government propaganda and that was responsible for a large portion of the mental deficiency of the people. Now the statue of the peasant woman in her stylized dress towered before them and, as night fell, her raised arm no longer seemed to be asking the nation to awaken from slavery; rather, it seemed to call down her anathema upon the infamous powers that extended far, very far throughout the world.

NOTE FROM THE
TRANSLATOR

The original title of this work is *Un complot de saltim-banques*. "Saltimbanque" is a lovely word, and Cossery, who carefully chose all his words, used it in this book in a variety of ways. The literal translation would be something along the lines of "street artist" or "street entertainer"; you can see images of *saltimbanques* in Picasso's "rose period" painting from 1905 entitled *Family of Saltimbanques*. The description of this painting that appears on the National Art Gallery's website reads in part:

> "From late 1904 to the beginning of 1906, Picasso's work centered on a single theme: the *saltimbanque*, or itinerant circus performer. The theme of the circus and the circus performer had a long tradition in art and in literature, and had become especially promi-nent in French art of the late nineteenth century. . . . Circus performers were regarded as social outsiders, poor but independent. As such, they provided a tell-ing symbol for the alienation of avant-garde artists

such as Picasso. Indeed, it has been suggested that the *Family of Saltimbanques* serves as an autobiographical statement, a covert group portrait of Picasso and his circle."

Except in the title, then, which was chosen by the publisher, I have retained the word in French wherever Cossery uses it. It existed in English at one point as "saltimbank," but whereas the Romance languages have kept it, it seems sadly to have fallen out of favor in English, like a trapeze artist tumbling from her trapeze, without a net.

I would like to offer my thanks to the co-conspirators / *saltimbanques* who helped make this translation possible, or better:

To Donald Nicholson Smith, Sarah Barbedette, Barbara Epler; to Guy Walter, Adélaide Fabre, Isabelle Vio, Emmanuelle Bellissard, and Cédric Duroux of the Villa Gillet; to Mona de Pracontal; to Bassem Shahin; to Liz McGill; to the Centre national du livre; to Fabrice Gabriel, Anne-Sophie Hermil, and Mathilde Billaud of the Book Office of the Cultural Services of the French Embassy in New York.

And finally, thanks, as always, to my parents, Connie and Elmer Waters, and to Gwenaël and Margot Kerlidou, my loves, my life.

—Alyson Waters